The Arabian Nights

written by Wafa' Tarnowska

illustrated by Carole Hénaff

Barefoot Books
Celebrating Art and Story

To Andrew, who loves good stories, and to my grandma Hanneh who showed me their beauty – W. T.

To my love, Flavio, and Noah: 'beautiful as the moon when it's full'. To Mathis the star dreamer. And with special thanks to Marlena Torzecka – C. H.

This book has been printed on 100% acid-free paper

Barefoot Books 124 Walcot Street Bath BA1 5BG

Graphic design by Michael Gibson/Love Has No Logic Design Group, Chicago, IL

Colour separation by Grafiscan, Verona

Printed in China by Hung Hing Off-Set Printing Ltd

ISBN 978-1-84686-121-5

This book was typeset in Majidah Potens, Pabst Old Style and Lynton BQ. The illustrations were prepared in acrylics

1 3 5 7 9 8 6 4 2

British Cataloguing-in-Publication Data: a catalogue record for this book is available from the British Library

Contents

Introduction

*T*he *Arabian Nights*, or *The Thousand and One Nights*, known in Arabic as *Alf Layla wa Layla*, is a collection of fables, fairy tales, adventure stories and historical anecdotes from across India, Persia and the Arab world. The stories were collected over several centuries by storytellers, authors, translators and scholars. The oldest Arabic manuscript (a few handwritten pages discovered in 1948) comes from Syria and dates back to the early 800s. The stories are also mentioned in Ibn Al-Nadim's *Fihrist* ('Catalogue of Books') in Baghdad in 938 AD. (The *Fihrist* was an index of all books written in Arabic during the Abbasid dynasty and kept in the 'House of Wisdom' in Baghdad.) A more substantial fourteenth-century Syrian manuscript, now in the Bibliothèque Nationale in Paris, contains some three hundred tales. Published in Arabic in 1984 by Muhnsin Mahdi and translated into English by Husain Haddawy in 1990, it is considered one of two definitive contemporary editions, together with the recent Penguin translation by Malcolm C. Lyons, Emeritus Professor of Arabic at the University of Cambridge. This edition forms the basis of my retellings.

Their roots may reach back for many centuries, yet the stories in *The Arabian Nights* continue to captivate readers of all ages. The beauty of these tales lies in the way they weave the extraordinary and the supernatural into everyday life. Ordinary men and women have extraordinary meetings with demons and genies, princes and princesses, ghouls and magicians. Kings and queens disguise themselves as ordinary people, leave their palaces to meet their subjects and learn to become better rulers. And through simple storytelling, Shahrazade, a beautiful and clever woman, changes an angry and violent man, Shahriyar, into a patient, generous and kind-hearted husband and father.

The Arabian Nights has become part of the world's cultural heritage. The tales have left their mark on music and painting as well as on common speech. The expressions 'open sesame' and 'genie', as well as images of flying carpets and magic lamps, are now widely used in films, television and children's books.

When I was a girl growing up in Lebanon, my grandmother Hanneh had only to say, 'Kaan ya maa kaan' in Arabic, or 'Once there was, and there was not…', for all the children to gather around to hear her retell a story from *The Arabian Nights*, embellished and modified according to her whims and to the time available, but always magical and memorable. Many of the stories she told had courageous heroines and princesses who helped their men in time of need, and these have influenced my selection. I believe that Hanneh had much in common with the heroines she described: the daughter of a village sheikh, she left her father's house as a bride decked with gold jewellery, sold every one of her bracelets and necklaces to educate her children, then used the rest of her dowry to dig a well in the house so that the family would have running water. I dedicate this book to her memory.

Wafá Tarnowska, Dubai, 2010

Shahriyar Meets Shahzaman

Long ago, when tales travelled along the Silk Road from China to Persia, crossing wind-blown sand dunes and busy oases, bleak mountain passes and fertile valleys, there lived two Persian kings of the Sassanid dynasty. They were brothers, and each of them was as handsome, brave and loving as the other. At the time of this story, it was ten years since their father's death, and ten years since they had last been together, for the old king had divided his land between the two of them and had sent them to live at the two ends of the empire to keep it together. One brother ruled from the city of Ctesiphon in the west and the other from Samarkand in the east, so neither saw the sun set at the same time as the other.

The elder brother was called Shahriyar. He was also known by his subjects as the 'king of kings' or 'shahanshah', shortened to 'shah'. The younger brother was called Shahzaman. He was referred to as the 'knight of knights', or 'fares al fursan', by his people. Both brothers had married for love, not for money or status, and both were blissfully happy with their wives. They were also kept extremely busy year after year dealing with affairs of state.

One day, Shahzaman woke up with a pain in his heart and tears in his eyes. He suddenly realised how much he missed his brother. 'Open my treasury and prepare my horses,' he told his men. 'Load the camels with precious gifts and food and water for the road. We are going to visit my elder brother Shahriyar in Ctesiphon.'

7

As the camels were being loaded and the horses groomed and saddled, Shahzaman went to his wife to kiss her goodbye. When he left her chambers, the scent of her rose perfume lingered on his robes. A few hours out of Samarkand, the scent reminded Shahzaman that he had left behind a special bottle of perfume he wanted to give to his brother, so he asked his men to continue the journey while he galloped back to the palace.

He quickly dismounted and slipped quietly through his wife's quarters so as not to disturb her. As he did so, he was horrified to see her embracing one of her manservants. The world turned dark before his eyes and the blood seethed in his veins. 'I have barely left my wife for a few hours and she is kissing another man!' he exclaimed. 'What else might she do while I am away?'

Then, wild with pain and fury, he drew his sword and killed them both. Without even pausing to wipe his sword, he grabbed the bottle of perfume, jumped back on his horse and galloped away to join the caravan.

Shahzaman did not breathe a word about what he had done to anyone. But his heart was so heavy with sorrow that he stopped eating. When the caravan finally reached Ctesiphon, his brother could hardly recognise him. Shahriyar was even more worried when his brother barely touched a morsel of food during the magnificent welcome banquet. Shahzaman's lips did not curve

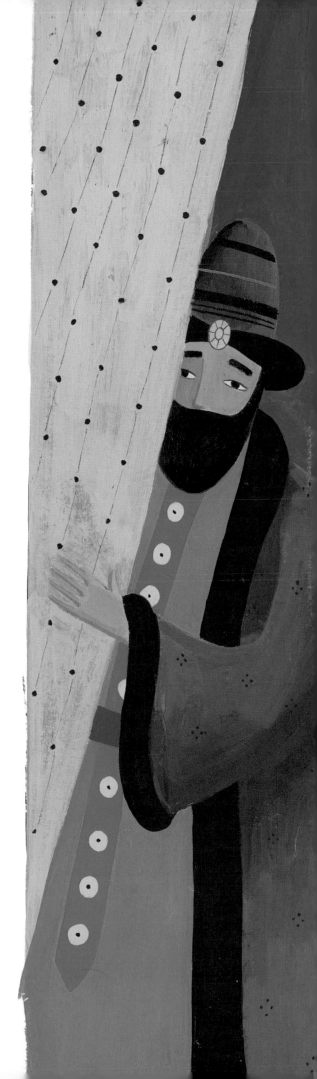

into a smile when his oldest friends came to welcome him; his eyes did not light up when his favourite childhood singer stepped forward to perform; and his hands did not clap in applause when his favourite tunes were played.

'Please tell me why you are so sad,' Shahriyar said to his brother at the end of the evening. When Shahzaman did not answer, he went on: 'I think you need some fresh air, so I am going to take you hunting with me tomorrow morning.'

When morning came, Shahzaman excused himself from joining the hunt. Instead, he asked his brother: 'May I stay in the palace for the day and stroll around the gardens?'

'By all means,' replied Shahriyar. 'We have a magnificent rose garden. We also have a beautiful orchard with all sorts of fruits for you to sample.'

As soon as Shahriyar left to join the hunting party, Shahzaman stood by the window of his room and thought of his wife. Despite the beauty of the secluded little garden below, he felt no pleasure in looking at it. Lost in his sorrow, he did not at first notice the queen, followed by ten of her maidservants, come through the gate of the garden and bathe in the marble fountain. A few minutes later, he heard the gate creak open and looked down to see a young army officer, as handsome as the moon, enter the garden and join the queen in the fountain.

9

He closed his ears so as not to hear the sound of laughter and splashing water, and his eyes so as not to see his brother's wife.

'Poor Shahriyar,' said Shahzaman to himself. 'He is just as badly off as I am. How can I tell him about his wife?'

Not wanting to hurt his brother's feelings, Shahzaman decided to say nothing. As the day passed, however, he started to feel better because he realised he was not the only man to have been betrayed by a woman. So when Shahriyar returned from the hunt that evening, Shahzaman was in a better frame of mind. His appetite had come back, he talked more freely and he applauded the musicians at the evening concert. He even smiled from time to time.

During the week that followed, Shahriyar observed how his brother's health improved. Full of curiosity, he took him aside and asked: 'Brother Shahzaman, if I ask you a question will you promise to answer me truthfully?'

'Of course, brother,' replied Shahzaman.

'Can you tell me what has brought on your sudden change of mood and your better health?' Shahriyar enquired.

Shahzaman explained what had happened with his wife on the day of his departure and how inconsolable he was for having killed her in a fit of anger. Shahriyar put his arms around Shahzaman's shoulders and said: 'Brother, I can now understand your sadness and your anger. But you have still not told me what has brought about your change of mood.'

And so, Shahzaman told him what he had seen in the garden. Shahriyar was stunned. 'I shan't believe you until I see it with my own eyes!' he cried.

'Very well,' said Shahzaman. 'Let's pretend to go away for a couple of days. Then, let us leave your men camping in the forest and return to the palace without anyone knowing. You will see for yourself whether I'm telling you the truth.'

Shahriyar Meets Shahrazade

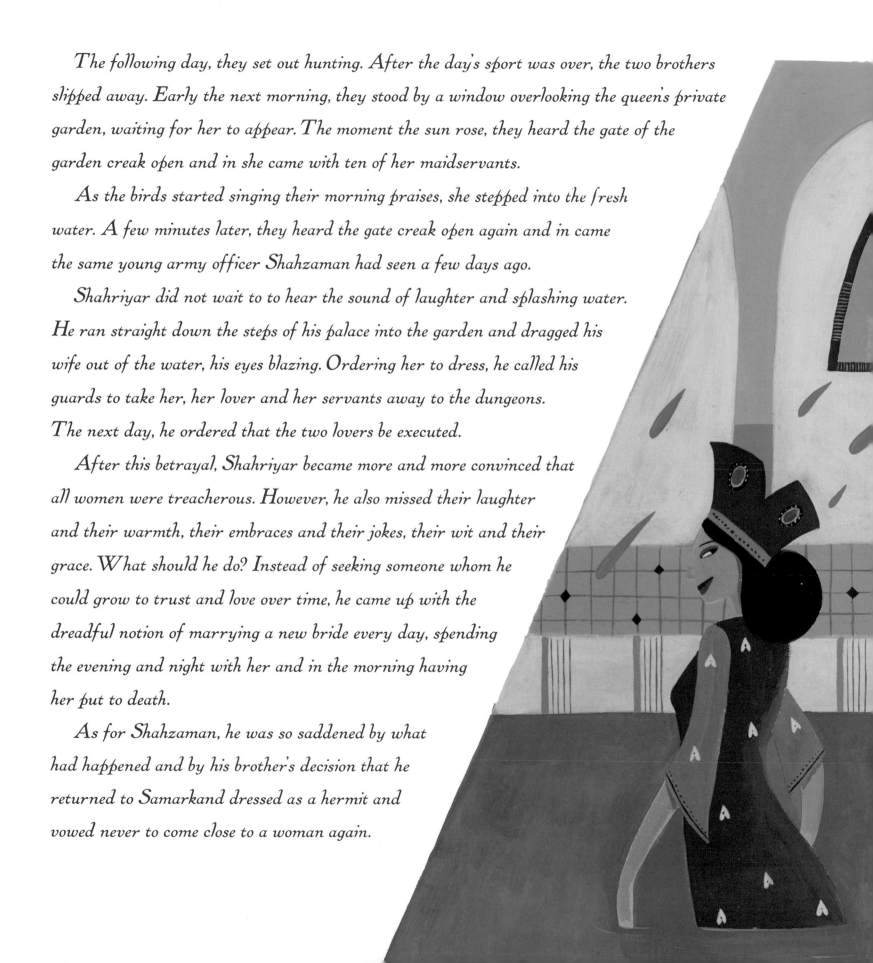

The following day, they set out hunting. After the day's sport was over, the two brothers slipped away. Early the next morning, they stood by a window overlooking the queen's private garden, waiting for her to appear. The moment the sun rose, they heard the gate of the garden creak open and in she came with ten of her maidservants.

As the birds started singing their morning praises, she stepped into the fresh water. A few minutes later, they heard the gate creak open again and in came the same young army officer Shahzaman had seen a few days ago.

Shahriyar did not wait to to hear the sound of laughter and splashing water. He ran straight down the steps of his palace into the garden and dragged his wife out of the water, his eyes blazing. Ordering her to dress, he called his guards to take her, her lover and her servants away to the dungeons. The next day, he ordered that the two lovers be executed.

After this betrayal, Shahriyar became more and more convinced that all women were treacherous. However, he also missed their laughter and their warmth, their embraces and their jokes, their wit and their grace. What should he do? Instead of seeking someone whom he could grow to trust and love over time, he came up with the dreadful notion of marrying a new bride every day, spending the evening and night with her and in the morning having her put to death.

As for Shahzaman, he was so saddened by what had happened and by his brother's decision that he returned to Samarkand dressed as a hermit and vowed never to come close to a woman again.

Shahrazade and Duniazad

A month passed during which time Shahriyar had already married thirty women and put each one of them to death. He had wedded the daughters of princes and merchants, officers and commoners — each of them just for one night. Each young woman was beheaded in the morning.

Fathers and mothers kept their daughters under lock and key so that the shah's soldiers would not take them to him. Whole families started leaving the city to protect their daughters from their unjust ruler, and prayers rose to Allah asking Him to deliver them from this evil.

But a whole year passed and no one could stop Shahriyar's madness. The thankless task of finding a new bride each night fell to his vizier. With every young woman he brought to the shah, the vizier's heart sank further because he knew that one day one of his daughters would have to be presented to his cruel master. The vizier was dreading that day because he had not one, but two lovely daughters, both of marriageable age. The elder was Shahrazade and the younger Duniazad.

Both daughters were as clever as they were beautiful, but of the many talents they each possessed, the most notable was Shahrazade's gift for telling stories. She loved telling them, reading them, collecting them and translating them, for she could speak several languages. She had collected stories from as

far away as China and India. Her mind was like a treasure trove and she
was full of invention too, making each story more elaborate than the next.

But imagine Duniazad's horror when one day she heard her elder sister
say to their father: 'Let me marry the shah!'

'Are you crazy?' the vizier exclaimed. 'Who in their right mind would
choose to marry him, knowing what lies in store?'

'Father, I have no intention of dying,' Shahrazade replied. 'Someone must
put an end to this madness and I believe I can do it.'

'I will not let you endanger your life,' concluded the vizier.

For many weeks, he would not let his elder daughter raise the subject
again. In the meantime, the city of Ctesiphon was in continuous mourning.
Young women were getting scarce and the army was becoming ruthless in
its search for suitable brides. The vizier, meanwhile, felt under increasing
pressure to lead by example. He could hear the courtiers whispering during
council meetings about how their daughters were being led to the slaughter
while those of the vizier were spared.

Finally, the vizier decided to give in to Shahrazade and let her have her
way. He and his wife wept all day as their beloved daughter was dressed for
the wedding. Even Shahriyar felt a tinge of remorse at marrying the child
of his trusted vizier, so he was unusually kind to her. Hence he did not say no
when she asked if her younger sister Duniazad could join them for the rest
of the evening so that she could tell her a story before going to bed.

'But there is a condition,' he said. 'I must be
free to listen too. What kind of story will it be?'
'The kind of story that entertains children and adults, kings
and queens, the rich and the poor, the kind of story your grandmother told
you when you were little,' Shahrazade answered sweetly.

Shahriyar remembered how when he was little his grandmother used to sit
him down at the end of the day and tell him tales of courage and bravery about his
ancestors, the kings of Sassan, and Ardeshir, the founder of the Sassanid dynasty.
'Maybe I should hear one of her stories to pass away the night,' he said to himself.

When Duniazad entered the royal bedchamber, she bowed to him, kissed
her sister Shahrazade on the cheek and asked her in a small, sad voice:
'Shahrazade, as this is your last night with us on this earth, can
you please tell me one of your best stories so that I might
remember you forever?'

Duniazad settled at her sister's feet while
Shahriyar stretched on his couch, put his arms
behind his head and felt himself relaxing for the
first time in a year. 'Maybe this bride will prove
different from all the others,' he thought to himself
as Shahrazade started talking.

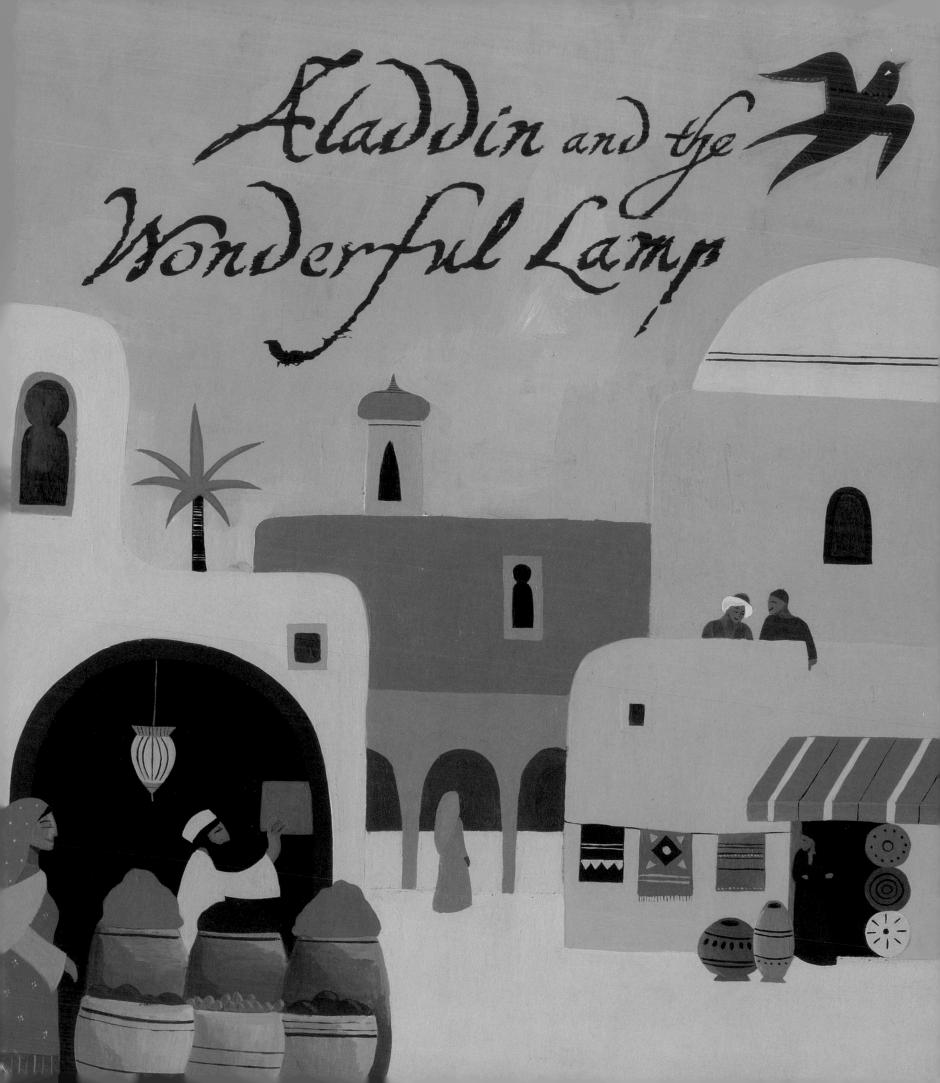

'Let us have a little more light', Sharazade suggested. Soon, the three of them were sitting surrounded by the flickering light of a hundred oil lamps. Shahrazade picked one up and quietly gazed at its dancing flame. 'You would be surprised, my lord, at how useful a lamp can be.'

'What do you mean?' asked the shah.

And so Shahrazade began her first story...

Aladdin and the Evil Magician

Once upon a time in a faraway land lived a mischievous lad called Aladdin. Aladdin and his mother only had each other for support, for Aladdin's father, Mustafa the tailor, had died when his son was just a child.

Aladdin's poor mother toiled day and night to feed herself and her son, mending clothes and spinning cotton. She barely earned enough to put one meal a day on the table. Aladdin was easily old enough to help her, but he was a layabout. He never did a stroke of work, preferring to roam the streets, playing pranks with other good-for-nothing youths.

Now one day, a tall, dark stranger came to the city where Aladdin lived. This man was an evil magician, well practised in the dark arts. During his long years of training, he had learned of a lamp, a lamp so powerful that its owner's every wish would instantly be granted. Of course, there was nothing the magician wanted more than to have this lamp for his own, so he had studied long and hard in his attempts to locate it. He now knew where it was hidden – and he also knew that to lay his hands on it he would need the help of a small, agile assistant. So he was on the lookout for a youth who was quick and bright and who would do anything for a bit of extra cash.

The magician bided his time, loitering in the shadows of the souk for a few days and watching all the comings and goings. It did not take him long to notice Aladdin because the boy was always harassing the traders, and he was quite a ringleader. So one morning, the magician

stopped a young lad, pressed a silver coin into his palm and, still gripping the boy's hand, murmured quietly: 'That youth over there, what can you tell me about him?'

'Oh! Don't you recognise him?' the boy asked. 'That's Aladdin, the son of Mustafa the tailor, who died a few years ago, peace be with his soul. I thought everyone knew him!'

Now the magician had the information he needed. He let go of the boy's hand, slipped away and waited for the right moment. Later that day, he saw Aladdin sitting by himself. He sidled up and asked, 'Are you the son of Mustafa the tailor?'

'Yes, sir,' answered Aladdin, 'but my dear father has been dead for a while now.'

'Ah, no!' cried the stranger, and he took the boy in his arms and started sobbing. 'I am your uncle, your father's brother, and I have not seen him for many years, for I make my living as a merchant and I have been travelling in faraway lands.'

Then he pulled two gold coins from the pocket of his silk jellabiya and pressed them into Aladdin's palm, saying: 'Go and tell your mother to prepare dinner.' And without even waiting for an answer, he vanished.

Aladdin and the Wonderful Lamp

Aladdin was reeling with shock but he ran quickly to his mother, shouting: 'Mother, mother, my uncle is back and he wants to meet you. He has given me a gold coin – can you please prepare something good for dinner?' (Aladdin, who never missed a trick, had already decided to keep the second gold coin for himself.)

'Uncle, what uncle?' demanded his mother. 'Your father never told me about a brother.'

'But this man knows my father's name and his trade and he is eager to meet you,' said Aladdin. 'Besides, he is rich. Can you please, please, please prepare a meal for him?'

'Well, why not?' said Aladdin's mother as she stared at the shining gold coin. 'After all, this will keep us warm and well fed for the next two months.'

That evening, the tall, dark stranger sat with his 'nephew' and his 'brother's wife' and enjoyed a delicious meal of rice and meat and pistachio nuts, all of it washed down with sweet pomegranate juice, and followed by yoghurt, dates and fragrant honey.

'So,' said the self-proclaimed uncle to Aladdin's mother, 'what future have you planned for this fine young man?'

'Well,' she sighed, 'your nephew likes to spend his days roaming the streets with his friends. His poor father tried everything to make him learn his trade, but Aladdin refused. Mustafa died broken-hearted, peace be with his soul, and to be honest I don't know what to do.'

'I understand,' said the so-called uncle, and he turned to Aladdin. 'How would you feel about my setting you up in a shop selling silk and cotton fabrics? Rich men and women will flock to your door. I can guarantee to supply you with the finest materials; you will be able to dress well and serve your customers apple tea. I see no reason why you should not make a decent living.'

'I would like that very much,' said Aladdin, full of excitement.

'Very well,' said the magician. 'Tomorrow morning is Friday, a day of prayer and rest. Wear this new jellabiya and I shall take you to visit some prospective clients after midday prayers.'

The next day, the magician led Aladdin outside the city, to the district where rich people had their country retreats. The two of them strolled from garden to garden, and the magician told Aladdin all about the different stages involved in making the exquisite clothes that the rich men, women and children were wearing. Aladdin was so excited, he did not notice that the magician was leading him further and further away from the city, deeper and deeper into the countryside.

In the afternoon, they stopped to share some dates, fruit and cakes and rest their feet. 'Isn't it time we went back?' asked Aladdin. He realised that he didn't know where he was, and he was starting to feel frightened.

'No, no, no – you must wait until you have seen the most wonderful garden of all,' replied the magician. He sprang to his feet and strode off. Aladdin put aside his fears and hurried after him.

They walked and walked until at last they came to a narrow valley between two high mountains. Here, the magician stopped and ordered Aladdin to gather wood for a fire. When the fire was lit, he threw in some incense and pronounced some powerful magic words.

Aladdin and the Wonderful Lamp

At this, a great cloud of smoke arose and the earth trembled. Aladdin trembled too! When the smoke had subsided, the magician pointed to a heavy stone slab with a ring in the middle of it. 'Now, my nephew,' he said in a stern and frightening voice, 'if you listen to me carefully and do exactly what I say, you will be handsomely rewarded. Disobey me and you will dearly regret it.'

'Yes, uncle,' replied Aladdin in a small, shaky voice.

'See this slab of stone down here. You alone shall lift it. Beneath it there is a narrow passage leading to three halls. Walk through each hall in turn without looking right or left. Do not even touch the walls. At the end of all three halls you will find a garden with the most marvellous fruit growing in it. Don't touch any of the fruit. Walk directly across the garden until you reach a terrace. There, you will see an alcove and in the alcove a small brass lamp shining in the dark.'

'I don't know if I can even lift this stone slab,' said Aladdin in a frightened voice, regretting ever having come on this journey.

'Don't interrupt me!' growled the magician. 'You will do as you're told. Take the lamp from the alcove in the wall and put the flame out. Empty the oil from it, put it in the pocket of your jellabiya and bring it straight back to me. You will be handsomely rewarded.'

'What if … what if something terrible happens to me?' asked Aladdin, his knees knocking.

'I have thought of that,' said the magician. 'Take this ring and put it on your finger. It will help you if you are in danger.' With this, he slid a ring off his little finger and gave it to Aladdin.

'Hurry now!' he ordered. 'It's getting dark.'

Aladdin put the magician's ring on his middle finger and pulled at the ring in the centre of the stone. To his surprise, he could lift it quite easily. Before him, as the magician had said, was a narrow passage with steps leading into a black hole. Aladdin took a deep breath and went down. After a while, he could see light ahead of him. The steps came to an end and he reached the first of the three halls. He hurried across each of them in turn, as instructed, without touching the walls. Finally, he arrived at the garden with the marvellous fruit trees. By now, he was starting to feel curious. 'I will taste some on my way back,' he thought to himself.

At the end of the garden Aladdin could now see a brass lamp glowing softly in an alcove. It looked utterly ordinary. 'Why all this fuss about a boring brass lamp?' he said to himself.

From far away, he could hear his companion calling: 'Have you found it? Have you found the lamp? Hurry! It is getting dark out here. Hurry back at once!' But Aladdin was not good at obeying orders. As instructed, he put out the flame and emptied the lamp of its oil before tucking it into the pocket of his jellabiya. But he dawdled on his way back, stopping to look at the fruit growing on trees and other plants.

He had been hoping to eat some, but close up they looked hard and shiny, not like any fruit he had ever seen.

'These are not real fruits, they are coloured stones,' he thought. He was surprised, for he had never seen a precious stone in his life, but he was right. The fruits of that magic garden under the earth were all made of gemstones: the figs were sapphires, the strawberries rubies, the pears topazes, the cherries garnets and the grapes amethysts.

'I'd better take some to my mother,'
he thought. 'She could probably sew them on some
of the dresses she sells.' So he filled his pockets with the
precious fruits. He also stuffed his wraparound silk belt with
silver plates and goblets from the treasure chests he saw in the halls.

'Hurry, hurry!' shouted the magician from the top of the steps. 'What's
keeping you?'

'I'm coming, I'm coming!' said Aladdin, tightening his belt.

'Bring that lamp up here, right now!' shouted the magician.

Then he lost his temper. 'This boy needs to learn to obey orders,' he
thought. So he took some grains of incense out of his pocket and threw
them on to the burning embers. Thick dark smoke billowed from the fire,
the ground shook and the stone slab rolled back into place.

Aladdin heard the rumbling above his head and the stone closing the entrance to the
cave. He was trapped! He felt weak with fear. 'I'll run back to the garden to see if I can
get out from the other side,' he thought. But the door at the far side of the three halls had
also magically closed. Aladdin sat on the steps underneath the great slab of stone and
started sobbing.

'Allah the Great, what is to become of me?' he cried, wringing his hands and rubbing
them together. As he did so, he rubbed the ring that the magician had given him.

In an instant, a huge genie rose out of nowhere, bowed in front of him and
said: 'Shabbey, Labbey, your slave is here to obey! I am the
genie of the ring, ask of me anything.'

Aladdin fell back in astonishment then, pulling himself together, he cried: 'Please get me out of here!' In a flash, he was transported out of the cave and found himself standing beside the remains of the fire. The magician was nowhere to be seen. He turned to thank his rescuer but the genie had disappeared. 'Allah be praised!' he said aloud before setting off back to the city. When he reached home he was so exhausted that all he could do was collapse on to his bed. Within seconds, he had fallen asleep. As she watched him, his mother noticed a dingy brass lamp that had rolled out of the pocket of his jellabiya.

'Why don't I clean this old dirty lamp and sell it at the souk?' she said to herself. The moment she touched it, a huge cloud of smoke rose out of the lamp and the tallest, roundest creature she had ever seen appeared before her and said in a deep, rumbling voice: 'Shabbey, Labbey, your slave is here to obey! I am the genie of the lamp, your wish is my command!'

Aladdin's mother fainted right away. But Aladdin, more accustomed to apparitions of this kind, woke up at once, grabbed the lamp from her hands and ordered: 'Bring us something delicious to eat.'

In an instant the genie produced two large silver platters filled with perfumed rice, tender roast lamb, a jug of delicious orange juice and two glistening silver goblets.

'Your wish is my command, master,' said the genie, depositing the plates and jug and goblets on the carpet. 'Do you need anything more?'

'Thank you,' said Aladdin. 'You may go back to the lamp now.'

'How can such a huge fellow fit into such a small lamp?' his mother asked when the genie had gone.

'The space inside it must be of a different dimension from ours,' said Aladdin.

After they had finished eating, Aladdin's mother suggested they sell one of the silver platters.

Over the next couple of months, Aladdin sold all of the silver platters and goblets, including those he had smuggled back from the cave.

With each visit to the souk, he learned more about the value of gold, silver and precious stones. He now understood that the coloured stones he had brought in his pockets from the cave were emeralds, rubies, sapphires and diamonds. So he put them in a strong metal casket which he kept hidden.

Over the next couple of years, Aladdin became quite rich, thanks to the genie of the lamp and his own skills as a merchant. He bought himself a nicer house and furnished it well. His mother was able to stop work and instead spent her time visiting friends.

One day, as he was walking in the souk, Aladdin heard the sultan's heralds shouting to the crowd: 'Make way, make way, lower your eyes: Princess Badr el Boudour, "Moon of Moons" and daughter of our beloved sultan, is passing here on her way to the hammam. If any man should dare to steal a look at the princess, he will be severely punished and regret the day he was born. Make way, make way, lower your eyes, lower your eyes!'

Aladdin, who never took any notice of orders, hid behind a big wooden door. He was determined to steal a look at the princess. And he was not disappointed. For as the convoy passed by, Aladdin peeped from behind the door and saw that Badr el Boudour herself was peering through the curtains of her palanquin to have a look around. She caught Aladdin's gaze and smiled back, her green eyes glittering with laughter. That was enough. Aladdin was smitten.

'Mother,' he announced when he returned home, 'I have fallen in love with Princess Badr el Boudour and I intend to marry her.'

'But my son,' she cried, 'this is pure folly! No son of a tailor, no matter how rich, can marry a princess. This is an impossible dream. It is time you found yourself a wife, though. In the morning, I shall go and ask my friends if they know of a more suitable bride for you.'

Aladdin and the Lovely Princess

Aladdin's mother tried to dissuade her son at first, proposing the butcher's daughter, the baker's daughter, even the goldsmith's daughter as alternatives. But Aladdin was as stubborn as a mule at the edge of a cliff.

'The only woman I shall ever marry is Badr el Boudour,' said Aladdin. And he locked himself in his room and refused to eat. 'Mother, you need to find a way!' he cried whenever his mother tried to tempt him back out. 'Do something or I shall die!'

So Aladdin's mother summoned all of her courage. The next day, she went to the sultan's majlis, taking as a present some of the precious stones, carefully wrapped in a silk cloth. She sat there all day in the sultan's court, waiting for her turn to be heard. But she was too modest to assert herself and step forwards, so her turn did not come – neither that day, nor the day after, nor the day after that.

After several days had passed, the sultan himself nudged his grand vizier and said: 'I have been noticing this woman dressed in black and clutching a bundle of silk. She has come every day for the past six days. Bring her over here so I might hear her plea.'

Aladdin's mother was shaking from head to foot. She threw herself at the sultan's feet. Then she raised her head and said: 'Sire, I am not even worthy of shining your sandals, let alone eating at your table, but my son Aladdin, son of Mustafa the tailor, has earned great riches. You would

not even know of him if he had not had the audacity to glance at your precious Moon of Moons, your daughter Badr el Boudour. Since that day, he has not eaten a crumb nor drunk a drop and he has begged me to bring you this modest gift in exchange for her hand.'

The sultan laughed loudly at the woman's boldness, but curiosity was nagging at him like an annoying fly. So he told her: 'I hope for your sake that this gift is worthy of the beauty and the rank of my darling Badr el Boudour, whom your son should never have seen in the first place!'

But the moment the sultan unwrapped the silken bundle, the precious stones shone with a radiance that took his breath away. 'These jewels are indeed worthy of my little princess,' he murmured, caressing them with his plump fingers. Then, turning to his vizier, he said: 'What do you think of this woman's demand, grand vizier?'

The grand vizier, whose honeyed tongue had enabled him to keep his post for many years, said as he examined the stones: 'They are indeed worthy of our beloved princess, sire. But she is not yet seventeen. Shouldn't you make her suitor wait for at least three months until she has finished preparing her trousseau?'

'You are quite right!' said the sultan. 'Tell this woman to return in three months.'

What the sultan did not know is that the grand vizier wanted his son to marry the princess and needed some time to bring the sultan round to this idea.

As for Aladdin's mother, she hurried back to her son to tell him the good news. Filled with joy, he immediately started dreaming of the palace he would build for his princess with the help of the genie of the lamp.

Two months passed, with Aladdin eagerly awaiting the day when he could claim Badr el Boudour as his bride. Then one afternoon, as Aladdin's mother was in the souk buying some

silk to make herself a new dress, the merchant asked: 'Are you buying silk to wear at the wedding feast of our princess and the son of the grand vizier?'

'The princess's wedding feast?' echoed the mother. 'I must tell my son at once.'

But it was too late, the princess was to be married that evening. 'I cannot believe the sultan has not kept his word!' cried Aladdin indignantly. 'I must stop this marriage at once!'

'My son, sometimes the wind blows the wrong way and the ship has to take a different course. Maybe you should just give up this foolish dream.'

'I won't give up this dream, mother – never,' said Aladdin, storming out of the room.

At the end of the wedding feast, and knowing that the bride and groom would have retired to their bedchamber, Aladdin rubbed the magic lamp. 'Bring the princess, her husband and their bed right here into this house,' he ordered the genie.

In an instant the wedding bed covered with rose petals landed in front of Aladdin with the princess and her groom sitting bolt upright, both looking terrified.

'Take the groom seven miles outside the city's gates and leave him there,' said Aladdin to the genie. The genie obeyed, and the poor groom spent all night walking back to the palace.

'My beloved,' said Aladdin, kissing the princess's hands, 'don't be frightened, just listen to my story. Your father promised me your hand, for two months ago I gave him the most beautiful gemstones in the

world. A promise is a promise. I am only doing this to win you back. Trust me.'

The princess wept at first but as she listened to Aladdin and looked more closely at him, she recognised the handsome young man she had seen in the gold souk. 'What shall we do?' she asked, for she knew she was in love with him and had no interest in sharing her life with the son of the grand vizier.

'Don't worry about a thing,' said Aladdin. 'For the time being, you must go back to your father's palace, but I shall see to it that we are brought together.'

The next morning, anyone who was out on the streets at sunrise would have been astonished to see a flying bed with a frightened princess on it speeding across the sky towards the palace. That same morning, the sultan and his wife woke up late after the wedding festivities and went straight to the princess's bedchamber to greet their daughter.

'So, did you spend a happy night, my darling?' asked the sultan.

'No, I did not!' the princess retorted, and just as she had finished speaking the dishevelled groom walked in, with muddy feet and a face like a thunder cloud.

'Where have you been, my son?' enquired the sultan, raising his eyebrows in surprise.

'Oh, just out for a little walk,' lied the young man.

For five nights in a row, the genie spirited the princess and her groom away from the palace. And for five nights in a row, the poor groom was left miles outside the city and had to walk for hours to get back. On the sixth day, he requested a private audience with the sultan.

Aladdin and the Wonderful Lamp

'I am deeply sorry, your majesty, but I cannot remain as your daughter's husband,' he said to the sultan. 'This marriage is already proving much too hard.'

The sultan was furious with the young man and immediately banished him, along with the grand vizier. 'You have both shamed me, and brought shame on my innocent daughter! This must be a lesson from Allah, blessed be His name. I should have kept my promise to the tailor's son. Guards, fetch me Aladdin at once!'

The moment Aladdin arrived at the palace, the sultan said: 'My daughter is yours, my son. You are far more worthy of her than the son of the grand vizier!'

'I am greatly honoured, your majesty,' Aladdin replied. 'For as long as I draw breath, your daughter will be the queen of my heart.' Then, pointing to a window in the audience chamber, he said: 'And this, sire, is where she will live.'

Following Aladdin's finger, the sultan caught sight of the most magnificent palace he had ever seen. The lamp had worked its magic: the domes of the palace were of red and its windows – ninety-nine in total – encrusted with crystals that reflected the sun's rays and changed colour with the time of day. The walls were of white stones, each carved by hand. The floors were of white marble and the pillars of jasper and agate. The furniture was of ornately carved sandalwood, draped with fine brocades. Every detail was exquisite.

'You are invited to visit your daughter's home this evening,' said Aladdin, smiling broadly. 'And I assure you, your majesty, that you will not be disappointed.'

'Allah is great,' said the sultan, embracing his new son-in-law.

The wedding feast was spectacular. Aladdin won the hearts of the people that night and before long everyone forgot about his bad behaviour as a youth. Everyone except the magician, that is. Far away in the depths of Africa, word reached him about the celebrations and the marvellous palace. 'I thought the young scoundrel was dead,' said the magician to himself. 'He must have escaped from that cave and discovered the magic of the lamp, for no human could have built that palace, certainly not overnight. I must get my lamp back!'

The Magician's Revenge

*I*t took months for the wicked magician to make his way to the city where Aladdin lived. By this time, the princess was expecting their first child and stayed mainly indoors. When the magician asked about Aladdin, he learned that he had gone hunting for a few days and was directed to the magnificent palace beside the sultan's. Seeing the palace for himself, the magician was quite convinced that Aladdin had the lamp. He now had to concoct a clever plan to retrieve it while Aladdin was away.

The next day, the magician, dressed in the shabby clothes of a street vendor and carrying a basket of shiny new brass lamps, stood under the windows of the palace and shouted at the top of his voice: 'New lamps for old! New lamps for old!'

One of the maidservants heard him and rushed to the princess, laughing and saying with tears of mirth in her eyes: 'Can you imagine the folly of this man, your highness, selling new lamps for old! I wonder how he makes any profit.'

The princess, who had a good heart and was always willing to help others, looked around the room to see if she could help the lamp seller. She then caught sight of the magic lamp sitting on a shelf, gathering dust. 'Why don't you take him this one?' she suggested to the maidservant. 'We never seem to use it.'

So the maidservant casually took the old lamp and handed it over in exchange for a new one. The magician could not believe his luck. He quickly rushed from the palace to the seashore, where he waited until night time. Then he took the lamp and rubbed it with a bit of sand. Immediately the genie appeared in a cloud of smoke, bellowing: 'Shabbey, Labbey, your slave is here to obey! I am the genie of the lamp, your wish is my command!'

'Here you are at last!' bellowed the magician in return. 'I have been waiting for you for so long.'

'Shabbey, Labbey, your slave is here to obey!' repeated the genie of the lamp.

'I order you to carry Aladdin's palace with the princess in it to my home in Africa.'

Within minutes, the beautiful palace with its red domes and crystal-encrusted windowpanes, not to mention a terrified princess, landed in the middle of the African jungle, followed by the wicked magician on a flying carpet.

The following morning, the sultan decided to call upon his daughter for breakfast. But, to his horror, there was no palace to be seen, let alone his darling Badr el Boudour.

'Bring me my son-in-law immediately!' shouted the angry sultan. 'Allah only knows what he's up to again,' he sighed, rubbing his face with his hands.

Aladdin, who had just returned from his hunting expedition, was speechless with shock as he rode towards the sultan's palace.

'Bring me back my daughter at once!' bellowed the sultan.

'Or you will pay for this with your life!'

'Give me forty days, my lord, and she will be back,' promised Aladdin. And without further ado, he galloped out of the city in search of his beloved princess.

That night, Aladdin stopped by a well to drink, wash and pray. As he rubbed his hands together, partly in prayer, partly in worry, he accidentally brushed the magic ring. Immediately the genie of the ring appeared and said: 'Shabbey, Labbey, your slave is here to obey! I am the genie of the ring, ask of me anything.'

'Bring me back my palace and my wife,' cried Aladdin.

'I cannot do so, master,' said the genie of the ring. 'Only the genie of the lamp can do that, for he is much more powerful than me.'

'Then take me to her immediately,'
said Aladdin, and within minutes he was flying
towards Africa on a magic carpet sitting beside the genie
of the ring.

As they landed beneath the princess's window, he heard her
shout: 'I shall not leave this room until you tell me what you've done to
my husband!'

'Your husband is dead and buried,' the wicked magician replied.
'Your father had him executed when you disappeared.'

'That's not true,' cried the princess. 'I am not leaving this room until
you give me proof of that.' And Aladdin heard the banging of doors as the
magician stormed out of the princess's quarters.

Aladdin was relieved to find his wife in such a combative mood. 'I must first go
and speak to her then work out how to get the magic lamp back,' he said to himself,
before summoning the genie of the ring. 'Take me to the princess,' he commanded, and in
an instant he was standing next to his wife, who almost fainted with joy to see him alive
and well.

'Shhh,' he whispered, kissing her hands. 'I am so glad you are unhurt. We must find
a way of getting the magic lamp back.'

'I have an idea,' said the princess. 'Why don't I pretend I have changed my mind
and let the wicked magician into my room, then offer him a drink with sleeping
powder in it?'

'Genie of the ring,' said Aladdin, rubbing his ring, 'bring me some sleeping powder
this instant.'

The genie obeyed at once, reappearing within seconds with the powder. Badr el Boudour asked her maidservants to prepare her the most delicious sherbet and slipped the powder into one of the cups. Then Aladdin hid in a cupboard and waited for the magician to return. Soon, they heard the sound of his footsteps as he approached the chamber.

'Princess,' he wheedled, 'I beg you to change your mind. This husband of yours is truly dead. I shall have the proof tomorrow morning.'

'If this is the case,' said Badr el Boudour in her sweetest voice, 'let me invite you in for a glass of sherbet.'

The wicked magician could not believe his luck, for when the princess finally opened her door she looked more beautiful than the moon, with a shimmering silver dress and matching veil.

'Welcome,' she said. 'Take this – you must be thirsty.'

'More thirsty for a sight of you,' he said, gulping down his sherbet, his eyes glued to her. After just a few mouthfuls, he was snoring away on the couch. The princess opened the coat covering his robe and found the magic lamp tucked away in one of the inner pockets.

'Aladdin, come here quickly,' she called. 'I have your lamp!'

Aladdin jumped out of the cupboard, took his beloved lamp and rubbed it at once. Out popped the genie, with his customary greeting: 'Shabbey, Labbey, your slave is here to obey! I am the genie of the lamp, your wish is my command!' Then he added: 'I am so relieved to be serving you again, sir.'

'Take us back, and the palace as well, but leave the magician here in the African jungle. We never wish to see him again.'

So the genie carried the palace and its inhabitants back, and as the sultan woke up that morning and looked out of his window, he was overjoyed to see his daughter and her husband walking towards his palace, smiling and holding hands.

'They're back, they're back!' said the sultan to his wife. 'Hurry up, my dear, and get dressed. I want to hear the full story!'

'You have truly excelled yourself, my dear,' said Shahriyar, embracing Shahrazade. 'It has been a long time since I have enjoyed a story so much. What other tales can you conjure for me?'

'You will have to wait until night falls again, my king,' she replied. 'For it is then that the loom of stories weaves its best designs.'

The Diamond Anklet

One night, as Shahrazade sat with Shahriyar at dinner, the tinkling
sound of the serving maid's anklets brought a smile to her face.

'What are you smiling about?' asked the shah.

'I am reminded of the story of an anklet — an anklet that belonged to a
beautiful and faithful woman called Zubaida.'

The Clay Jar

Zubaida was the youngest of three half-sisters and the most beautiful. The three girls were born of different mothers and when their mothers died, the sisters lived alone. Zubaida worked as a carpet weaver. She sat at her loom every day with a smile on her face and a tune on her lips, while the most intricate designs sprang from her nimble fingers. Her two sisters did nothing. They simply spent the money Zubaida earned.

Also, the two elder sisters were jealous of Zubaida's beauty. In truth, she was simply remarkable, with long brown hair that swayed like palm leaves and green, almond-shaped eyes. Her lips were as bright as the ripe seeds of a pomegranate and her feet as delicate as a gazelle's. What is more, she had a lovely personality. She was also the best carpet weaver in town, working from morning until night without a word of complaint.

Although Zubaida's carpets fetched a lot of money in the souk, her sisters only let her keep a few dirhams with which she bought flowers for her room or a comb for her hair or a piece of cake, for she was often hungry.

One day, Zubaida met a strange old man in the souk. He wore a simple turban and had a long white beard. As she walked past him he urged her to stop, holding out a small clay jar. 'This little pot will bring you happiness, my child,' he said.

'How can a simple clay jar bring happiness?' asked Zubaida with a laugh as she offered him her dirhams.

'Just take it home and you will see,' said the old man mysteriously.

Back home, Zubaida put some flowers in the jar and returned to her carpet weaving. She was now feeling hungry, regretting having spent her money on a vase rather than something to eat. 'I wish …' she began.

The words were hardly out of her mouth when she heard a deep voice inside the jar saying: 'Ask for what you wish and you will have it.'

Zubaida jumped straight off her stool. She rushed to the jar and turned it round and round, but she could not see anything in it except her flowers and the water. 'I must be hearing things,' she told herself. 'I haven't eaten for two days. I wish I had enough money left for a date cake.'

The moment she said the words 'I wish,' some delicious date cakes appeared in front of her, served on the most exquisite silver platter. Zubaida could not contain her joy. She started to twirl around the room with her platter of freshly baked cakes.

Then she sat down to eat them quietly before her sisters returned from the souk.

From that day on, Zubaida's life started to change. Whenever her sisters went out, she asked the genie in her little clay jar for special favours: dresses, shawls and jewels; delicately embroidered slippers; delicious dishes of rice and meat; and the best woollen threads with which to weave her carpets. She always made sure she shared her gifts, however, distributing them among her neighbours. She also made sure she kept the magic jar secret from her sisters, changing back into her old and tattered clothes before they came home.

One day, the king decided to invite all the young people of the kingdom to his palace to celebrate his son's coming of age. The ladies were invited to the women's quarters and the men to the great hall to meet their future ruler.

'You cannot come wearing those worn-out old clothes,' her sisters told Zubaida. 'You would shame us all. You had better stay here, taking care of the house instead.' And they rushed to prepare themselves for the party, leaving poor Zubaida lost for words. But the moment her sisters had left, she went straight to her faithful little clay jar. 'Please make me a dress the colour of the moon,' she whispered. Immediately, a shimmering silk robe appeared, with a matching veil and slippers.

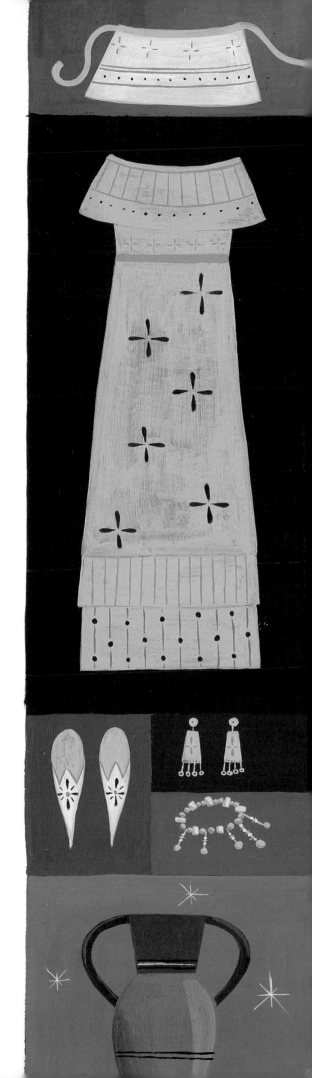

'All I need now is some beautiful diamond anklets and bracelets to look like a real princess,' she told her jar. And sure enough they too appeared. When she put them on, they made the loveliest tinkling sound.

Zubaida hurried to the party. When she entered the women's quarters, all of the ladies of the court gasped with admiration. 'Who is this mysterious lady?' they asked each other. 'Where does she come from?' Even her sisters did not recognise her behind her fine veil. She, of course, recognised them immediately because they looked like a pair of gaudy parrots in their bright, mismatched outfits.

Zubaida spent the time talking to the ladies of the royal household, asking discreet questions about the young prince and keeping as far away from her sisters as possible. She soon learned that he was an outstanding young man, hard-working and generous, and that his favourite pastimes were hunting, playing polo and chess. She tasted delicious foods served on silver platters, drank from crystal goblets and danced to the tunes of an orchestra made up entirely of women. While she danced everyone noticed her diamond anklets and bracelets, which sparkled at every step.

Zubaida almost forgot the time, so happy was she. But suddenly she overheard her sisters saying their loud goodbyes to the prince's mother. She hurried to a side door and ran as fast as she could down the palace steps to reach home before them.

She took off her anklets to avoid making any noise, but in her haste she dropped one of them into a water trough by the palace stables. Then she hurried home, hid the dress under her bed and pretended to be fast asleep.

The Diamond Anklet

'You missed an amazing party,' drawled the two sisters the following morning. 'There was this mysterious lady with a dress the colour of the moon and she danced like a gazelle and charmed all the ladies of the king's household. You should have seen the jewellery she had on,' they sighed. 'It would take you a lifetime of weaving to be able to afford just one of those anklets she had on her feet. By the way, shouldn't you be working now?'

As Zubaida sat at her loom working away and dreaming of the magical evening at the palace, the prince's groom brought one of his master's horses to have a drink at the water trough. The moment the horse saw the shining anklet in the water, he raised his head and neighed in fright, refusing to drink. The groom looked into the trough and spotted the diamond anklet. He picked it up, wiped it on his sleeve and took it straight to the palace.

'Ah!' said the prince's mother. 'There was a lovely young woman with a dress the colour of the moon and beaded silver slippers. She danced like a gazelle. I seem to remember she was wearing diamond anklets, just like this one.'

'Mother!' cried the prince. 'You must find her for me. She could be the bride I am looking for!'

'Let's not rush things, my child,' said his mother. 'She could be, but we won't know until we see her. I shall ask, let your father order a search for the mysterious lady who has lost this anklet.'

So the king sent the royal guards together with the royal maidservants to knock at every door in the kingdom. 'I think we are wasting our time in this home,' sighed one of the maidservants when they reached Zubaida's house. 'No one in a place like this could possibly own a diamond anklet.'

But she was interrupted by
the two sisters sticking their heads through the
door. 'Come in, come in,' said the pair of them, bowing
obsequiously. 'We have been expecting you all day.' That morning
they had washed their feet with rose water and rubbed almond oil on
them to make them smooth. They had not moved from their sofa, so as
not to miss the visit.

The royal maidservants tried to attach the anklet to the first sister's
ankle, then to the second sister's, but with no success. The sisters held their
breath, pulling the anklet as tight as it would go, but the clasp would not
reach – their ankles were too thick!

'Don't you have another sister?' asked one of the maidservants, who
happened to know the family well. 'The one that makes beautiful carpets.'

'What do you want with her?' said the sisters. 'She never leaves her loom, and
besides she has the ugliest feet you've ever seen.'

'The prince has instructed us to try the anklet on all the women of the
kingdom,' replied the royal maidservants, 'and he means everyone. Go and fetch
your younger sister, please!'

So they did. You should have seen the look of horror on their faces when they
found Zubaida wearing her moon-coloured dress and her beaded silver slippers.
The maidservants instantly remembered the beautiful young woman who had
danced so well at the party. Of course, the anklet was just the right size and made a
perfect pair with the one Zubaida already had on.

The White Dove and the Poisoned Pins

The maidservants wailed with joy and declared Zubaida to be the eagerly-awaited royal bride. Leaving the older sisters gaping, they escorted her to the palace. The king and queen were captivated, as was the prince, who fell instantly in love with her, and arrangements were made for the royal wedding to be held without further delay.

Now, as everyone in the kingdom was preparing for the wedding celebrations, Zubaida's two sisters were searching her room inch by inch for the secret of her moon-coloured dress and her jewellery. All they could find was the old clay jar on the windowsill and some jewellery she had hidden under her mattress.

'Let's pretend to be happy for her and take her belongings to the palace,' said one sister to the other. 'Maybe we shall discover her secret that way.'

Zubaida welcomed her sisters with open arms, for she was a forgiving person as well as being deliriously happy. She insisted that they come to the wedding and she even offered to have special dresses made for them.

'We are very grateful for your generosity, little sister,' they cooed. 'We are truly happy for you, and wish you a wonderful life with the prince. We have just one question. Do you still need the little clay jar in your room and the jewels we have found under your mattress?'

'You can keep them all. I have no need of my little clay jar any more now that my prince will provide for all my needs.' Then, wanting to make them feel a little less jealous of her good fortune, Zubaida blurted out: 'I can even tell you the secret of the jar!' And with that, she explained about the genie in the jar that had granted her every wish.

The Diamond Anklet

Now the sisters had everything they needed. The moment they returned home, they asked the magic jar for half a dozen poisoned hairpins, decorated with diamonds.

On the morning of the wedding, the two sisters took their poisoned gift to the palace in a beautiful golden filigree box and presented it to Zubaida. 'We were hoping to put them in your hair ourselves,' they told her, in their sweetest voices.

'Of course, dear ones,' said Zubaida good-heartedly. But the moment the first pin touched her scalp, Zubaida felt dizzy. When the second one touched her, she fainted into her sisters' arms. The malicious pair continued planting the pins into their sister's hair. They did not manage to kill her, though; instead, the poison transformed her into a white dove with six diamond pins hidden under the soft white feathers of its head.

'There,' cackled the wicked sisters, after they had finished their gruesome task. 'Go and marry your prince now!' The dove flew out of the window and perched on top of a nearby tree, trembling with fear. Then the sisters threw open the doors of the dressing room and ran towards the palace guards, shouting and weeping and tearing their clothes. 'Help, help, the bride has disappeared!' they cried.

The guards searched the palace but with no success. The king dispatched his soldiers to the furthest frontiers of the kingdom but with no success either. The queen's maidservants were sent again into every home to look for Zubaida, but she was nowhere to be found.

The prince fell sick with heartache. He stopped eating; he no longer went hunting or played chess or visited his friends. He just sat by the window of his room and prayed to Allah for the safe return of his bride. His only comfort was a beautiful white dove with soft, shiny feathers, which cooed on his windowsill.

One morning as the dove lingered by his window, the prince gently caressed its soft head. It did not fly away; on the contrary it stood still, as if wanting more. So he caressed its head again, until his fingers touched something hard.

'I must find out what it is,' he told himself. He gently lifted the feathers on the dove's head and saw six shiny diamonds stuck deep into the bird's scalp. As he lifted the first one, the dove fainted in his hands but he continued to remove each pin in turn. As he did so, the dove slowly transformed itself into a beautiful young woman. When the last pin came out, he realised he was holding none other than his beloved Zubaida!

'I have finally found you, my love,' he murmured. 'This time I will never let you go.'

While the palace renewed the preparations for the wedding, Zubaida told the prince her story. He immediately dispatched the royal guards to seize the sisters and to collect the magic jar. 'What shall we do with these jealous women now?' he asked.

Zubaida answered: 'Let me ask the clay jar.'

By now, the genie living in the jar was utterly worn out from having to indulge every whim of the two greedy sisters. By way of a reply, he simply stretched out his arms, caught one sister in each arm and pulled them into the jar, swallowing them both in one big gulp.

'We shall put this jar on the top shelf of the treasury,' the Prince declared. 'With the poisoned pins inside,' he added. 'No one will disturb it, I am sure, for our treasurer has better things to do than notice an old clay pot.'

The day of the wedding ceremony was declared a national holiday, and Allah gave the prince and his bride many happy years together as well as half a dozen children – three boys and three girls. The children loved nothing more than listening to the story of how their parents met and playing with their mother's diamond anklets.

'And they never asked about the clay jar?' said Shahriyar.

'Of course they did,' replied Shahrazade, 'but their parents told them that they had thrown it to the bottom of the sea.'

'Let us stroll along the shore tonight,' said Shahrazade to Shahriyar.
'Tonight my story is inspired by the sea. Come, let us watch the summer
stars and the moon reflected in its waters.'

The Girl from the Sea

In a city of ancient Persia there once lived a great shah. He was a wise and good man who ruled justly, so that all his subjects wished him a long and happy life.

Now, this shah was blessed in every way except one. He had no wife, and no heir. He prayed every day for a woman who would give him a son or daughter, but although at the time of my story he was already growing long in years, he had not yet met anyone with whom he felt he could share his life. Then one day a merchant from a distant land came to the city and everything changed.

The merchant entered the royal palace bringing with him a slave girl whom he wished to present to the shah. When the girl was brought before him, the shah was speechless, for she was as beautiful as the rising moon and as slender as a reed. Her silky black hair fell down her back. Her cheeks were as lustrous as ripe pomegranates and her dark eyes shone with warmth.

The good shah's heart trembled. 'How much do you want for this girl?' he asked.

'I have been travelling for over a year to present her to your majesty,' answered the merchant, 'and I paid a very high price for her. I am asking you for two thousand dinars, sire.'

'That sum does not reflect her true worth,' declared the shah. And turning to his vizier, he said: 'Give this man not two but ten thousand dinars, and while you're about it, make sure he gets a new robe and a decent meal.'

The merchant bowed low, kissed the shah's hand and left.

The shah gave the slave girl the best rooms in the palace. For reasons he could not quite explain to himself, he felt sure that she would be happiest in rooms overlooking the sea. When he paid his first visit to her, she was indeed standing by the window, staring out across the

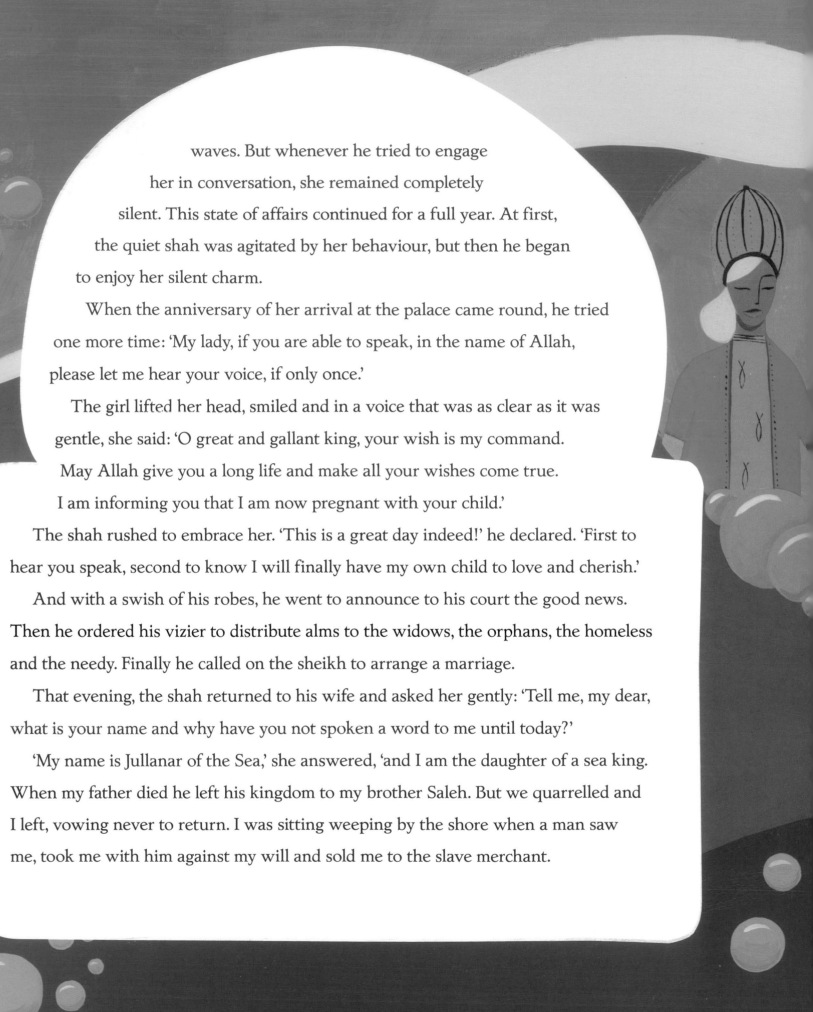

waves. But whenever he tried to engage her in conversation, she remained completely silent. This state of affairs continued for a full year. At first, the quiet shah was agitated by her behaviour, but then he began to enjoy her silent charm.

When the anniversary of her arrival at the palace came round, he tried one more time: 'My lady, if you are able to speak, in the name of Allah, please let me hear your voice, if only once.'

The girl lifted her head, smiled and in a voice that was as clear as it was gentle, she said: 'O great and gallant king, your wish is my command. May Allah give you a long life and make all your wishes come true. I am informing you that I am now pregnant with your child.'

The shah rushed to embrace her. 'This is a great day indeed!' he declared. 'First to hear you speak, second to know I will finally have my own child to love and cherish.'

And with a swish of his robes, he went to announce to his court the good news. Then he ordered his vizier to distribute alms to the widows, the orphans, the homeless and the needy. Finally he called on the sheikh to arrange a marriage.

That evening, the shah returned to his wife and asked her gently: 'Tell me, my dear, what is your name and why have you not spoken a word to me until today?'

'My name is Jullanar of the Sea,' she answered, 'and I am the daughter of a sea king. When my father died he left his kingdom to my brother Saleh. But we quarrelled and I left, vowing never to return. I was sitting weeping by the shore when a man saw me, took me with him against my will and sold me to the slave merchant.

The rest of the story you know. If you had not been so kind to me during this past year, I would have returned to the sea.'

'But my dear, why did you wait so long to tell me all this?' asked the shah.

'I wanted to make sure that you would be a good father to this baby. Now I know that you will. And as my confinement is near, I feel I should like my mother and brother by my side. May I invite them to come and visit?'

'Of course,' the shah replied. 'Invite them here immediately.'

So Jullanar removed a bead of her pearl necklace, threw it into the fire, then muttered a magic incantation in a language her husband could not understand. The sea outside the window started to foam and billow and out of the waves emerged an elegant old lady, a handsome man and five beautiful maidens. These were Jullanar's mother, brother and cousins. The shah was not expecting them to arrive quite so suddenly, but he nonetheless enjoyed getting to know his exotic new relatives.

When the baby was born, it was a beautiful boy. Jullanar's mother bathed him and dressed him and carried him through the palace to present him to his father. The shah was so happy that he knelt down and thanked Allah in front of the whole court.

'Badr will be his name,' he said, 'for it signifies the moon and he is as beautiful as the moon when it is full.' Then he declared there should be forty days and forty nights of celebrations. It was the happiest day of his life.

On the fortieth day, as Queen Jullanar was sitting with her husband and family, playing with the baby, her brother Saleh took the child in his arms, twirled him around the room and cooed to him in a strange language. Then, taking everyone completely by surprise, he flew out of the window and disappeared with the baby into the sea. The shah felt the world turn dark before his eyes and let out a loud cry: 'Bring him back, bring back my son!'

'Do not fear, great king,' said Queen Jullanar. 'My brother will not harm the child.'

So they sat waiting by the window, silently praying for the safe return of their child until they heard the sea foam and surge and looked to see the boy's uncle appearing out of the waves holding the baby in his arms. Thanking Allah silently, they waited until Saleh was back in the room before asking him to explain himself.

'I hope you were not frightened, your majesty,' said Saleh, bowing before the shah as he passed the infant back to his father.

'I certainly was!' exclaimed his brother-in-law. 'Can you please explain to me the reason for your strange behaviour?'

'I went to the sea to draw around my nephew's eyes with special kohl blessed by the words inscribed on the seal of King Solomon, son of David,' replied Saleh.

Queen Jullanar then explained to her husband how, whenever a child was born to the people of the sea, the parents drew around its eyes with this special kohl in order to ward off evil.

Now Saleh took a purse from his pocket and emptied it in front of the shah, scattering scores of emeralds, rubies and diamonds at his feet, and saying: 'Brother-in-law, these gems are gifts for your son Badr from his uncle Saleh. May he never be in need.'

The shah was deeply touched by the generous gift and invited Saleh to extend his stay, but his guest replied: 'The kingdom of the sea awaits me. I cannot leave my subjects for too long. However, you are welcome to stay with us whenever you want, and we shall gladly come and visit you as often as we can.' With that, he and his mother and five cousins took their leave.

BADR

There were many visits from the people of the sea while Prince Badr was growing up. The years flew by and soon he was a fine young man, handsome, clever and courteous. He spoke many languages and chanted verses of the Koran exceptionally well. He was also an excellent rider, archer, sailor and poet.

When Prince Badr turned eighteen and had learned all that was needed to be a good king, his father summoned his court and announced to them he was ready to retire and that Prince Badr was to be his chosen heir. Badr was as good a ruler as his father, dividing his days between sporting pursuits and affairs of the state. Like his father before him, he often travelled through the cities and provinces of his kingdom, listening to his subjects and helping them.

But not long after he had become shah, Badr was called back to the palace with the news that his father was dying of pneumonia. The old shah just had time to give his son one last blessing before he passed peacefully away.

55

Princess Jawhara and the White Bird

When Badr turned twenty-one, his uncle Saleh came to visit him, bearing magnificent presents of coral and pearls. A sumptuous party was held and everyone danced all night until dawn. As the guests took their leave, Saleh approached Queen Jullanar to speak with her privately, and they withdrew to her quarters.

'My dear sister,' he said. 'Don't you think it's high time we found your son a bride? He is your only child and if anything happened to him the kingdom would be in great danger, and so would you.'

'Who do you suggest, my dear brother?' asked the queen.

'There are many worthy princesses in the kingdom of the sea,' answered Saleh. 'However, I think that none is more worthy of my nephew than Princess Jawhara, daughter of the powerful but ill-tempered King Shamandal.'

'Describe her to me,' said the queen.

'She matches your son in beauty and talent. She has no equal among the princesses of the sea or the land. Her teeth are like pearls and when she smiles the sea anemones open their petals and the fish dance in the water,' replied Saleh.

'Now I remember who she is,' said Jullanar. 'Her mother used to be my friend when I was a child. I think that your suggestion is perfect, dear brother. How shall we introduce them to each other?'

'First, we have to convince Jawhara's father to give his daughter to your son,' said Saleh. 'He has a reputation for being vain and tyrannical. I suggest we don't tell Badr about our plan just yet.'

What they did not know was that Badr had overheard their conversation. Too excited to sleep after the party, he had taken a walk in the garden. Hearing voices coming from his mother's sitting room, he had hidden by the window and listened. The description of Princess Jawhara's beauty roused his curiosity, and when his mother had retired to bed, he could not resist accosting his uncle: 'I beg you to take me with you tomorrow to the kingdom of the sea so I can meet this princess.'

'Didn't your mother teach you not to listen to people's conversations behind closed doors?' Saleh admonished him.

'Dear uncle, I know I am in the wrong,' replied Badr. 'Forgive me but I could not sleep – I was still excited after the party so I took a walk in the garden to calm myself. I heard your conversation by chance. Please take me with you tomorrow to the kingdom of the sea.'

'In that case, we must tell your mother at once,' said his uncle.

'Let's not worry her unnecessarily,' said Badr. 'I shall leave a message with my vizier that I have gone on business for a few days.'

At dawn the next day, Badr strode down to a sea that was as blue as lapis lazuli. His uncle arrived soon afterwards and the two men embraced. 'Take this ring,' said Saleh to his nephew. 'It will protect you from evil.'

With these words, he took his nephew by the hand and walked with him into the waves. They soon disappeared, swimming down and down until they reached Saleh's kingdom.

'Welcome to the kingdom of the sea, grandson,' said Saleh's mother. 'Come and warm yourself with some tea and tell us your news.'

'Guess what?' said her son teasingly. 'Your grandson is in love!'

His mother raised an inquisitive eyebrow: 'Aha! And may I know with whom?'

'With none other than Princess Jawhara, daughter of the wicked King Shamandal,' replied Saleh.

'She is indeed matchless,' said his mother, 'but it won't be easy to win round her father. I know what we can do, however. I shall go to the treasury and choose a selection of our finest jewellery and offer it to King Shamandal. I am sure this will help open his heart towards us.'

The next day, Saleh and his mother set out for the palace of King Shamandal. They took with them six seahorses carrying caskets filled with precious jewels and a retinue of one thousand men, partly for show and partly for protection.

'I have come to ask for your daughter's hand for my nephew,' said Saleh, saluting King Shamandal. 'And as a token of our esteem, my mother has chosen to offer you some of the finest jewels in our treasury,' he continued, kneeling to present Shamandal with one of the caskets.

'My daughter is not for sale,' snapped the king. 'And she does not need any of your jewels,' he added, dismissing them with a wave of his hand. His guests had no choice but to leave.

Saleh was fuming, however. 'I cannot tolerate such insulting behaviour from another person, let alone a king!' he exclaimed. 'What would my subjects think? That they can also be rude to me! This man has offended me and I shan't tolerate it.' With these words he summoned the soldiers of his retinue and ordered them to storm the palace, taking Shamandal prisoner.

As for Princess Jawhara, when word reached her that her father had been taken captive, she fled with her favourite maidservant. A small fishing boat took the two of them to a nearby island where the princess had once spent her childhood summers. There she hid in a tree house.

Meanwhile, when Badr's grandmother and uncle did not return, he decided to go and look for them. He chose to make the voyage in a small fishing boat and rowed for several hours until Fate brought him to the very island where Princess Jawhara was hiding. He even took a nap underneath the tree house!

When he woke from his sleep, Badr looked up through the tree branches to see a lovely face peering down at him. 'This beauty matches exactly the description my uncle gave of Princess Jawhara,' he thought to himself. 'Or it must be her sister or her first cousin. She truly is perfect.'

After an embarrassed silence, he said to the face peering down from the tree: 'Hello! My name is Badr. What's yours?'

'My name is Jawhara and I am the daughter of King Shamandal. Our palace has been overtaken by a strange army and my father imprisoned. I have had to flee with my maidservant to this island, taking refuge in this old tree house.'

'Princess Jawhara?' thought Badr, unable to believe his ears. 'I am sure it is my uncle Saleh's army that has conquered her palace. How can I ask for her hand now?' Then, plucking up his courage, he said: 'Princess Jawhara, I fear this is all my fault. My uncle Saleh had gone to ask for your hand on my behalf. Now I hear that he has taken your father prisoner and conquered your palace. I am truly sorry.'

'What does it matter whether you are sorry or not!' retorted Princess Jawhara, who was beside herself with rage and despair at this turn of events. 'It is clearly your fault that my beloved father is a prisoner and I am homeless.'

'Let us go and tell my uncle to release your father,' said Badr, by now totally smitten.

As she glared back at him, Jawhara formed a plan. 'First, you will have to climb up here and help me down,' she said, 'then perhaps we'll see if we can resolve this little difficulty.'

But as soon as Badr touched her hand, her face became as cold as marble and she said in a strange, harsh voice: 'Away from me, enemy! Lose your human form and become a bird!'

With these words, Badr was transformed into a beautiful bird with a blue beak and blue feet, perched shivering on a branch of the tree.

'Catch him at once!' Princess Jawhara commanded her maidservant, 'and take him to the Dry Island where he will die slowly and painfully of hunger and thirst.'

But the maidservant, who secretly felt sorry for Badr, took him instead to the Isle of Plenty. Here a multitude of fruit trees grew, watered by the sweetest of streams. 'At least you shall be well fed here, my handsome one,' said the girl, caressing the bird's head.

The Queen of the Isle of Plenty

Badr, transformed into a bird, was let loose on the Isle of Plenty. His distraught uncle searched for him everywhere, and so did his grandmother. As for his mother Jullanar, tired of waiting for him to return, she plunged into the sea and swam to her mother and brother to ask if they knew of her son's whereabouts.

'I am so sorry, my dear sister,' said Saleh. 'I should have told you about our plan to visit the kingdom of the sea. Badr was so insistent on not telling you. I truly regret having listened to him.'

Then he told her the story of the failed marriage request and of Badr's mysterious disappearance. 'There is no point in you waiting for him here, dear sister,' he went on. 'You should go back to Persia and govern the kingdom while he is away. I am sure that Allah in his infinite wisdom will guide you.'

So Queen Jullanar took leave of her brother and mother, and returned to Persia to wait for her son, taking over as ruler of the country in his absence.

As for Badr, he spent his days pecking at fruits and learning how to live in the wild, until one day a hunter trapped him in his net and put him in a cage. 'What an exquisite bird,' he thought to himself. 'I must take it as a present to the king.'

The King of the Isle of Plenty was captivated by the bird. He fed him at his table and was astonished to see Badr eating like a human: hopping from plate to plate, choosing the most tender morsels of meat and rice, even pecking at the dessert!

'What a strange bird,' the king told his wife. 'He eats everything I eat. How do you explain that?'

The Queen of the Isle of Plenty looked closely at Badr and said: 'This bird is not a bird but a human. Someone must have cast a spell on him.'

'Madam,' said the king, 'you cannot be serious!'

'I am perfectly serious, my lord,' she replied. 'This is Shah Badr of Persia and his mother is Queen Jullanar of the Sea. Follow me to my rooms and you will see.'

'My dear, you never cease to amaze me even after all these years,' said the king, following his wife.

The Queen of the Isle of Plenty was in fact a powerful magician. She was so moved by the plight of handsome Shah Badr that she decided to free him from the spell. So she took a copper vessel, filled it with water and pronounced some magic words over it. The water began to boil, bubble and steam. The queen then sprinkled some of the water on to the feathers of the shivering bird. In an instant, the blue feathers fell off and Badr returned to his human form. He fell on his knees to kiss the hands of the powerful queen, while the king looked on in amazement.

'Come, let us sit and enjoy a refreshing cup of sherbet,' said the king, 'while you tell us what we can do to help you.'

'I should be grateful for a boat to take me back to the land of Persia, where my absence must have caused great pain to my mother and disruption to my kingdom,' said Badr.

'Your wish shall be granted,' replied the king, ordering one of his newest ships to set sail with his best captain and sailors.

For the first ten days all went well, and the ship sailed smoothly across a sea that was as bright and calm as a mirror. But on the eleventh day, the wind changed and a storm arose, tossing the ship in all directions until it hit a rock and split in two. Some of the sailors drowned;

the others, including Badr, clung to
pieces of wreckage until they reached the shore.

Badr dragged himself onto the sand. 'Thanks be
to Allah,' he thought, 'I am back on dry land.' As he lay there,
exhausted and hungry, he looked around and saw, rising before him,
the walls of a great white city. Passing through the city gates, Badr was
struck by all the animals wandering around – horses, asses, cows and camels
– and scarcely a fellow human being. At every step, one of these creatures
would stand directly in his path, as if deliberately blocking his way.

'What is wrong with these animals?' he said to himself.
'And why are they wandering about the streets and not out in the
countryside where they belong?'

Finally, he came across an old man sitting by his vegetable stall and
smiling kindly through his wrinkles. 'Good day to you, uncle,' said Badr,
saluting the man.

'Good day to you, handsome youth,' said the old man, who was struck
by Badr's good grace and pleasant demeanour. 'What brings you to our
shores? Can I offer you a cup of sweet tea?'

Exhausted from lack of food and sleep, Badr sat by the vegetable
stall, sipping the delicious hot tea, and told the old man his story.

'Praise be to Allah,' said the old man, whose name was
Abdallah. 'Your mother must have prayed hard for you to have
escaped evil so often.'

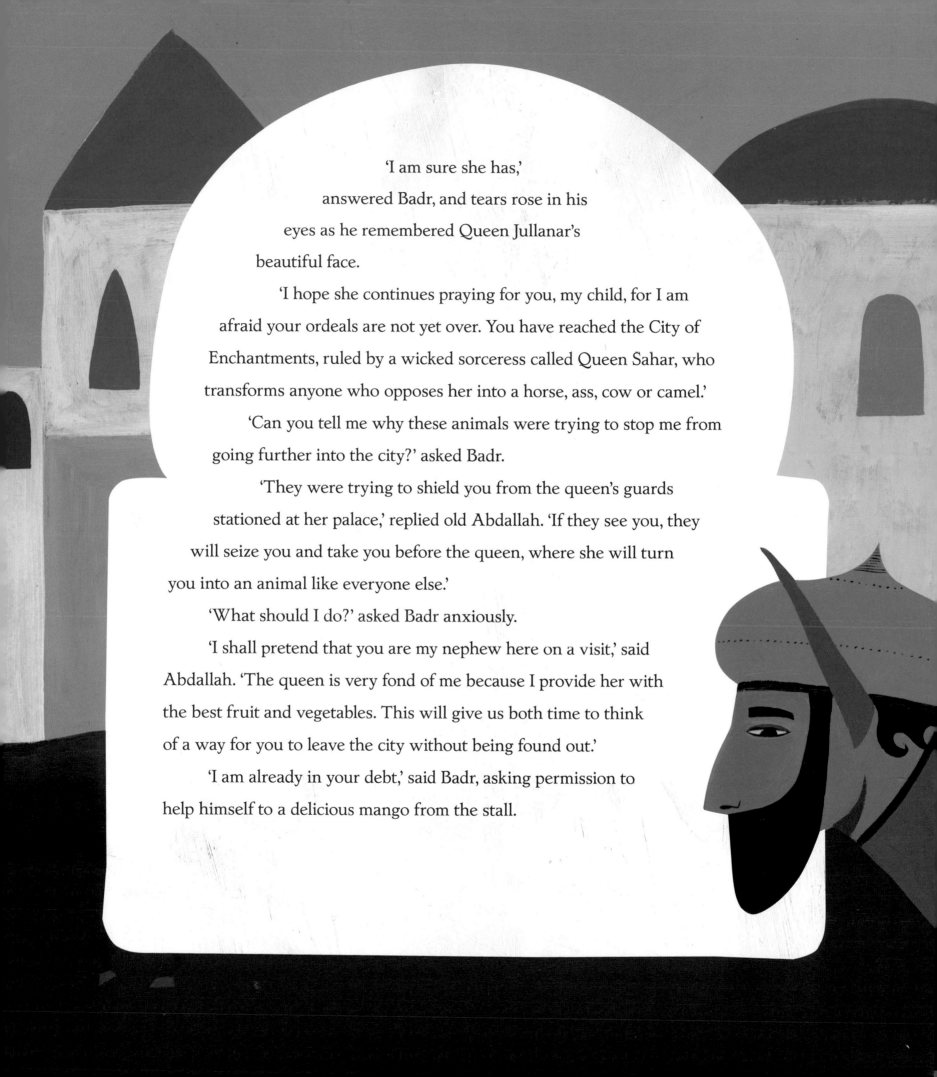

'I am sure she has,' answered Badr, and tears rose in his eyes as he remembered Queen Jullanar's beautiful face.

'I hope she continues praying for you, my child, for I am afraid your ordeals are not yet over. You have reached the City of Enchantments, ruled by a wicked sorceress called Queen Sahar, who transforms anyone who opposes her into a horse, ass, cow or camel.'

'Can you tell me why these animals were trying to stop me from going further into the city?' asked Badr.

'They were trying to shield you from the queen's guards stationed at her palace,' replied old Abdallah. 'If they see you, they will seize you and take you before the queen, where she will turn you into an animal like everyone else.'

'What should I do?' asked Badr anxiously.

'I shall pretend that you are my nephew here on a visit,' said Abdallah. 'The queen is very fond of me because I provide her with the best fruit and vegetables. This will give us both time to think of a way for you to leave the city without being found out.'

'I am already in your debt,' said Badr, asking permission to help himself to a delicious mango from the stall.

The Queen of the City of Enchantments

A month passed before Sahar, Queen of the City of Enchantments, realised she had a visitor. During that time, Badr lived with old Abdallah like a son, helping him run the stall, preparing his meals and sitting with him back home in the evenings, recounting the stories that his mother Jullanar had told him as a child.

One afternoon, as Queen Sahar was taking her monthly stroll in the market, she stopped by Abdallah's stall and so came face to face with Badr. 'Tell me, Uncle Abdallah, who is this handsome young man?' she asked in her sweetest voice.

'This is my nephew, your majesty,' answered the old man. 'My late brother's son, who has come to visit me after his father's death.'

'I wish to invite him to my palace for a meal,' said the queen.

'But of course, your majesty,' replied Abdallah, knowing full well that it was impossible to contradict her.

'I shall send my men at noon tomorrow to escort him,' said the queen with a smile.

'Your invitation is a privilege and a delight,' lied old Abdallah.

As soon as the queen had disappeared from view, he apologised to Badr: 'My son, it is impossible for anyone to refuse the queen. She is a most powerful sorceress. I advise you to keep your eyes and ears open and use your wits. Never underestimate the power of clear thinking,' he added, giving Badr a hug to reassure him.

The next morning, Queen Sahar dispatched her men to collect Badr. He rode through the streets on a magnificent stallion with a white star on its forehead. As he passed, people – those

66

who hadn't been transformed into animals – stopped whatever they were doing and gasped in admiration, for Badr was truly as beautiful as the full moon and he rode like a king. Riding by, he could hear the remarks of the crowd – 'Poor man, does he know how cruel and wicked our queen is?' or 'Will anyone deliver us from her evil?', and so on – until he arrived at the palace, where he was received with great pomp and given a place of honour at the queen's banquet. After the meal, Badr was shown to a comfortable guest room and invited to stay for the evening concert when, he was told, the most talented musicians and poets would sing to the guests or recite poetry.

In this way, a routine started which continued for many days: in the early morning, a walk in the palace gardens with the queen, followed by a delicious breakfast; at mid-morning, riding in the nearby hills; then lunch, then a siesta, then card games and chess, then dinner and a concert.

After a month, Badr had changed his mind about the queen, in whom he only saw goodness. 'I don't understand what the fuss is all about,' he told himself, as he prepared for their morning stroll.

On that very morning, the queen had dispatched a servant to say that she was indisposed and could not

join her guest for their walk. So Badr

went off by himself around the gardens until he

reached the queen's quarters. Standing to one side of the

tall windows, he peeped inside and saw her kneading bread with

flour she had ground and had kept locked away in a special box, along

with a secret assortment of spices and other magical ingredients.

'This is what I shall feed you tonight, you handsome and foolish youth,'
she was chanting again and again.

A cold chill ran through Badr's spine. He returned at once to his rooms,
saddled his horse and said to his servant: 'Please inform the queen that I am
missing my uncle Abdallah so much that I must visit him instantly. I shall
be back this evening.'

'Dear uncle,' he said, as he dismounted, 'I saw something I should not have seen.
The queen was kneading bread in her room and singing as she worked. Do you have any
idea what this bread is?'

'My son, you are very wise to have come away,' replied Abdallah. 'The bread is
magical. She feeds it to people to transform them into horses, asses, cows or camels.'

'What can I do?' asked Badr, panicking. 'She is expecting me back to dine with
her this very evening.'

'Don't worry,' said old Abdallah with a smile. 'She is not the only one in this town
who can make magic bread. Come, roll up your sleeves so that you too may learn.'

So Badr helped old Abdallah knead and bake several small loaves of bread to
which the old man added a good dose of his own magic, for he also was a sorcerer who
knew how to use his skills when the occasion demanded.

'Here,' said Abdallah, presenting a basket full of bread to Badr, 'take these loaves and offer them to the queen at tonight's meal. But remember! Do not eat one morsel of her bread; instead, tease her and cajole her until she accepts some of yours.'

'Thank you, uncle,' said Badr, hugging his old friend. 'I shall see you tomorrow.'

'May Allah protect you, my son,' said the old man.

When Badr reached the palace, the queen was waiting for him impatiently. 'What took you so long?' she asked.

'I apologise, your majesty,' he replied. 'I have been helping my uncle to bake bread for you. He wishes to thank you for your hospitality towards me.'

'But we have so much bread in the palace,' said the queen, frowning. 'I too have baked some fresh loaves this very morning.'

'Ah! I bet they are not quite as delicious as my uncle's,' said Badr, with his charming smile. 'Can you please try one? They are hot from the oven.'

'No, no, no — I had much rather you try mine,' insisted the queen.

'Of course,' answered Badr, pretending to eat the crust but secretly slipping it into his pocket.

Then, pouring some water from a jar into the palm of her hand, the queen sprinkled it on to Badr's face and said: 'Be transformed into an ugly, limping donkey this instant!'

But nothing happened, and Badr continued smiling at the queen. 'What was that you said?' he queried innocently, eyes wide.

'I was just joking,' she said with a shrug.

'You frightened me for a moment, your majesty,' said Badr, offering her one of his loaves. 'Now it's your turn to taste some of Uncle Abdallah's delicious baking.'

This time the queen could not refuse. But the moment she swallowed the bread, she began to writhe like a serpent. 'What have you put in this bread?' she hissed. And before Badr could answer, she had become a beautiful mare.

'I think I prefer you this way,' said Badr, laughing. 'And I'm taking you to my uncle immediately.' With these words, he put a bridle around the mare's neck and dragged her kicking and neighing back to old Abdallah's vegetable stall.

'Vile sorceress!' said Abdallah when he saw the mare. 'You finally got what you deserve.' Then, turning to Badr, he said: 'My lord, you have no reason to stay in this city a moment longer. Mount the mare and go back to your kingdom. Your mother and your subjects need you.'

After embracing the old man, Badr rode for three days until he came to a city where an old man with a white beard invited him to have a glass of lemonade and take a rest. Being a trusting person, Badr accepted the old man's hospitality. An old woman served them. When she saw the beautiful mare, she exclaimed: 'Young man, please sell me this mare. It looks exactly like the one my son has lost.'

'Old lady,' said Badr politely, 'this mare is not for sale.'

'Not even for one thousand gold pieces?' she asked.

Badr laughed: 'Maybe one thousand gold pieces would make me change my mind.'

At that, the old woman unwrapped her belt and took out one thousand shiny gold pieces.

'I was just joking,' said Badr.

Upon hearing this, the old man said: 'Didn't you know, young man, that in our town no one is allowed to lie, even in jest? Our word is our bond – if you value your life, you must sell the mare for the price you have agreed.'

So Badr reluctantly took the money and gave the mare away. The moment the old woman had picked up the reins, she embraced the mare, whispering: 'My daughter, my darling, I have missed you so so much.' Then, sprinkling the mare with water, she ordered: 'Return to your human shape.'

The Queen of the City of Enchantments appeared instantly and hugged her mother. Badr could not believe his eyes nor fully understand how cleverly he had been tricked until he heard a low whistle and a huge genie appeared. 'Ladies, I am in your hands,' the genie announced, bowing in front of the two women.

'Take us to the City of Enchantments,' ordered Queen Sahar. Within minutes, Badr was flying on the genie's shoulders back to the city. As soon as they alighted at the palace, the queen sprinkled him with magic water and said: 'Leave your human shape and become an owl this instant!'

Within seconds, he had been transformed into an owl with hooded eyes.

'Put him in a cage and starve him to death,' ordered the queen.

Mercifully, the maidservant who took Badr away was also a good friend of old Abdallah. She fed the owl and gave it water, then secretly went to see the old man to tell him what had happened.

'It's time to use my magic again,' said Abdallah. He then gave a whistle and a huge genie appeared in front of him, saying: 'Shabbey, Labbey, your servant is here to obey.'

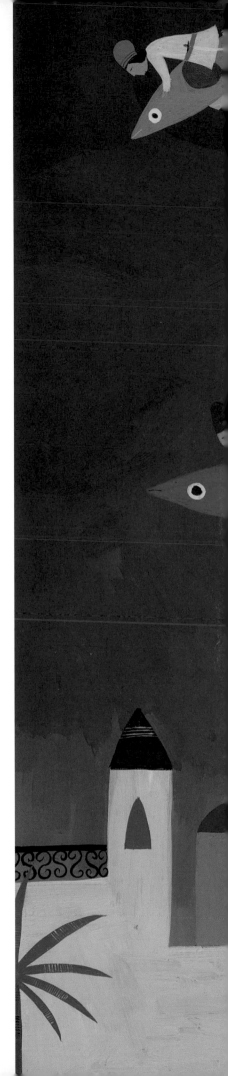

'Lightning!' Abdallah commanded, for this was the genie's name. 'Go at once to Persia and inform Queen Jullanar that her son is a prisoner of the Queen of the City of Enchantments. Let her gather an army of sea people to rescue her son from this evil woman.'

'You say and I obey,' Lightning the Genie answered.

Queen Jullanar was so overjoyed to hear that her son was alive that she went straight to her brother's kingdom. There, they summoned an army of sea people who rose up into the air and flew behind the genie to the City of Enchantments. The army surrounded the palace of Queen Sahar and defeated her men by storming the tower where the cage of Shah Badr was kept.

'My poor son,' said Queen Jullanar, trembling with relief and rage as she opened the cage. 'What have they done to you?' Then, taking some magic water into her hands, she sprinkled it over the owl, which was instantly transformed back into human form.

'Let us go straight to old Abdallah to thank him for his help,' said Jullanar, weeping with joy. 'We must also reward Queen Sahar's maidservant for saving your life.'

When these duties had been performed, Queen Jullanar flew back to Persia with her son Badr, carried by Lightning the Genie and followed by the army of sea people.

After a week of celebrations, Queen Jullanar took her son aside: 'My son, I am getting old and I wish to see you married and with children. We need to try once more to find you a bride.'

'Mother,' answered Badr, kissing Queen Jullanar's hand, 'I want to make you happy, but if the truth be told, I am still in love with Princess Jawhara whose father is a prisoner of Uncle Saleh.'

'Let me see what I can do,' said the queen.

'Saleh,' she told her brother a short while afterwards, 'I want you to convince this prisoner of yours to give his daughter's hand to my son. I am getting old and I wish to see Badr married and with children before I say goodbye to this world.'

'Dearest sister,' said King Saleh, 'you deserve to be a happy grandmother.' With these words, he disappeared into the sea and went to talk to King Shamandal, who had become much better tempered, and considerably more likeable, after his spell in prison.

'Would you consider having your kingdom returned in exchange for the hand of your daughter to my nephew, Shah Badr?' asked Saleh.

'I admire your persistence,' smiled King Shamandal. 'But what if she says no?'

'It is up to you to convince her,' said Saleh to his prisoner.

Princess Jawhara loved her father, but she was secretly very taken with Badr as well, so she was only too happy to help her father regain his kingdom. 'I must be precious to be worth a kingdom,' she whispered to Badr as he was slipping the wedding ring onto her finger.

'You are my most precious jewel,' he replied as he embraced her. 'The queen of my heart and of my kingdom.'

'Did Shah Badr and Princess Jawhara have many children?'
asked Shahriyar.

'Allah granted him half a dozen children and his reign was
remembered as a time of great peace and prosperity,' Shahrazade
answered with a smile.

The Ebony Horse

'This story,' said Shahrazade to Shahriyar one cool autumn night,
'is about a Persian prince, a Yemeni princess and a magnificent horse.'

The Marvellous Gift

The prince's adventures began one afternoon in early autumn. It was the habit of his father, Shah Sabur of Persia, to open the gates of his palace twice a year, for the spring and autumn festivals. During these celebrations, the streets were sprinkled with rose petals, sweets were given to the children and everyone dressed in their finest clothes. Shah Sabur opened up his kitchens and his treasury, distributing food and money, dispensing justice and accepting greetings and gifts in return.

On this particular occasion, an Indian magician, skilled in making curious and rare inventions, was among the crowds. The magician presented the shah with an extraordinary gift. It was a full-sized wooden horse carved in such a manner that it looked almost alive. Its coat shone, black as ebony, and it wore a finely crafted saddle and bridle, inlaid with golden studs and glittering jewels. Everyone marvelled at its beauty.

'Tell me,' asked Shah Sabur, 'what is the purpose of this object?'

'Your majesty,' the magician replied, bowing low, 'when you mount this horse, it will carry you up into the air and take you wherever you want to go. Moreover, in a single day it will travel farther than you and I could travel in a year.'

The shah was no fool, so he invited the magician to give a demonstration. And it was true! The horse could fly right around the palace. No one had ever seen anything like it. 'What would you like in return for your gift?' asked Sabur. 'You may have whatever you wish for.'

Now, the magician had heard of the
beauty and grace of the shah's youngest daughter.
So he told Sabur: 'If you are truly pleased with my gift,
your majesty, my wish is to ask for your youngest daughter's
hand in marriage.'

But the princess, who had been following the discussions
from the women's quarters, was horrified, because the magician
was old and ugly, with a nose like an aubergine and lips as pendulous as
those of a camel. She ran straight to her room and threw herself on her
bed, sobbing loudly. Her brother, who had just returned from a hunting
expedition, heard her cries and rushed to her room. She told him everything.

The prince, whose name was Kamar el Akmar, or 'Moon of Moons', went
straight to his father and confronted him. The shah shrugged. 'Don't worry about your
sister,' he said. 'Her suitor is quite worthy of her, no matter what he may look like.' Then
he showed his son the remarkable ebony horse and introduced him to the magician.

The prince was enchanted. He mounted the horse straight away. 'How does it work?'
he asked, as he swung into the saddle. But the magician, who was worried by this turn
of events, simply gave an enigmatic smile and a deep bow. He was right to be concerned,
for as soon as Kamar el Akmar picked up reins of the horse it started to fly. Up, up, up it
rose, above the roofs of the city, high into the sky, and over mountains, hills and valleys.
Within a matter of minutes, the prince had disappeared from sight.

'Bring him back!' demanded the shah.

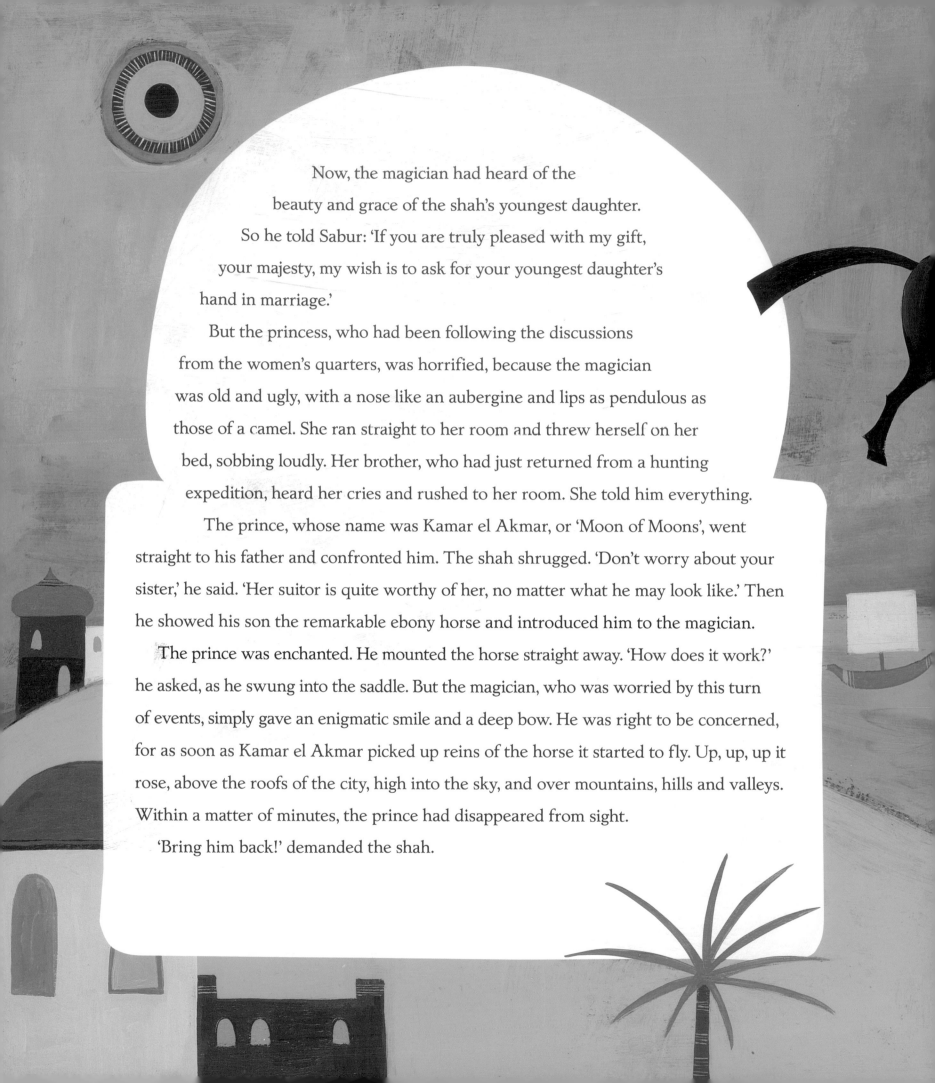

But the magician shook his head. 'Alas, your majesty, I cannot,' he replied. 'Your son is too impulsive. He has let the ebony horse fly too high and too fast. There is nothing I can do.'

Then the shah flew into a rage. He called his guards and had the magician taken to the dungeons.

At first, Kamar el Akmar was very excited by the novelty of the flying horse. Then, realising he knew neither how to bring it down, nor turn it around nor stop it, he began to panic. But being a courageous and resourceful young man, he did not completely lose his nerve. Instead, he started twiddling the horse's ears. He soon discovered that by doing this, he could control the horse, making it fly up and down and in different directions. Down he flew, and as he drew closer to the earth he saw a magnificent palace surrounded by battlements and protected by many guards, dressed in chain mail and armed to the teeth.

'Hurrah!' he thought. 'This looks like a good place to stop.' But wanting to evade the guards, he decided to land on top of the palace rather than risking the ground. So he steered the horse onto the roof. Then he went down one of the palace staircases, looking for food and drink as he had not eaten since the morning. Passing through a magnificent courtyard, he saw a light and went towards it. There he found a guard sleeping in front of a door, his hand on his sword, his provision bag hanging beside him. The prince quietly took the bag off its hook and ate its contents, then he took the guard's sword and opened the door quietly. The guard continued to snore away.

In the room, Kamar el Akmar was astonished to find a beautiful princess. She lay asleep on an ivory bed inlaid with jewels and draped with silk curtains embroidered with thousands of tiny pearls. He was so amazed at her loveliness that he spent a long time just gazing at her. Then he could not resist any more. He drew back one of the curtains, leaned over and gave her a kiss on the cheek.

Straight away, the princess woke up and she was about to scream when she realised that the person standing by her bed was the most handsome young man she had ever seen. So she quickly recovered her wits, asked him who he was and sat up to listen to his story.

When Kamar el Akmar had finished, the princess – whose name was Shams el Nahar, or 'Day Sun' – introduced herself as the daughter of the King of Sanaa, in Yemen. Kamar el Akmar had flown a long way south in just one day!

Hearing voices in the bedchamber, the princess's handmaids all woke up and raised the alarm. Kamar al Akmar was seized by the palace guards and brought before the king.

On learning that the intruder was a prince, the king was courteous to his unexpected guest and offered him a room for the night. But he was also so upset by the poor security in the palace that the next morning he challenged Kamar el Akmar to prove he was indeed a king's son by fighting his whole army. Without a moment's hesitation, Kamar el Akmar accepted, so the king ordered his commander in chief to prepare for battle. The army arrived on horseback, in full armour.

Seeing so many soldiers lined up outside the palace, Kamar el Akmar told the king: 'It seems unfair that I should fight your army on foot when your men are all mounted on horses. I ask permission to use my horse, your majesty.'

The king agreed to this, and Kamar el Akmar raced up the stairs to the roof, sprang into the saddle of the ebony horse and started twiddling its right ear. His mount swayed backwards and forwards and made the strangest movements, then it began to rise, gliding slowly over the palace. The soldiers were so stunned by the sight of the flying horse that they forgot to draw their weapons. By the time they had realised what was happening, the prince was high in the sky, waving down at them.

'Catch him, catch the rogue!' cried the king. But his advisors restrained him. 'Let him go, let him go,' they said. 'He must surely be a magician or a genie, so good riddance to him!' As for Shams el Nahar, she took to her chambers, refusing food and drink – for she had fallen deeply in love.

Kamar el Akmar flew like the wind until he reached his father's palace. Alighting on the roof, he saw that the stairs were strewn with ashes. 'Oh! Someone important must have died,' he thought. When he entered the throne room, he found his entire family dressed in black and weeping for him, for they thought he had gone for ever. They rushed over to him, their tears of grief turning to tears of joy. Hugging and kissing him, they sat him down to a good meal, demanding to hear all about his adventure. The prince then told them of his encounter with the beautiful Shams el Nahar, daughter of the King of Sanaa, and of how he had narrowly escaped being killed by her father's army.

While they sat there, eating, drinking and rejoicing, Shah Sabur asked one of the court singers to entertain them. She sang a poem of love and remembrance, her words moving Kamar el Akmar so much that he suddenly longed for the princess. So the moment the meal was finished, he excused himself. He climbed to the palace roof, mounted the ebony horse and flew all the way back to Yemen. There he found Shams el Nahar confined to her bed, pale and weak. She had not eaten a morsel since he had left.

Kamar el Akmar knelt at the princess's side and promised that he would come and

visit her every week. But this was not

enough for her. 'Take me with you,' she pleaded.

'I cannot live without you any more.' Then Shams el Nahar

packed a casket, put on her loveliest silk dress, wrapped

her head and shoulders with a delicately embroidered shawl and

quietly slipped away with Kamar el Akmar to the palace roof. The two

of them mounted the ebony horse and flew back across the starry sky to

the kingdom of Persia.

As the young couple galloped through the night skies, Kamar el Akmar

thought to himself: 'I must show the princess how much I value her. I cannot

just take her to the palace without warning my parents. I should go alone

to my father and announce her arrival properly.' So he brought the ebony

horse down to land at a small summer palace outside the city gates. Here, he kissed

the princess's hands and begged her to rest after the long journey. Then he hurried

away to announce his news and to organise a procession of welcome.

The Mad Princess

*N*ow we must turn to the magician, who had been released from prison following the prince's return. Having given up all hope of marrying the shah's daughter, he was determined to recover his precious ebony horse. Walking by chance by the summer palace, he saw the horse come down to land and couldn't believe his luck. 'Let me go and see if my hands can touch what my eyes have just seen,' he muttered to himself.

The princess did not like the look of the magician one little bit. His expression was sly and his ugly face and big nose made her shudder. 'Don't be afraid, your highness,' he purred. 'Prince Kamar el Akmar has sent me because I am the only one other than him who can fly the ebony horse. Besides,' he continued, in his most syrupy voice, 'he wouldn't want to send a handsome young man to accompany you on this journey, would he?'

'I suppose you are right,' conceded the princess. Then, against her better judgement, she climbed on to the ebony horse with the magician behind her. No sooner had they begun to fly over the city than she saw a magnificent procession coming out of the shah's palace with a splendid litter mounted on top of an elephant. This must be the welcome procession, she realised. For a moment, she thought that the magician would bring the horse down to meet them, but to her horror the horse started flying higher, away from the people below.

'Stop, stop, you wicked man! What are you doing?' cried the princess.

'I am taking you away from the prince, who tricked me and took my horse from me. I am now your master!' said the magician.

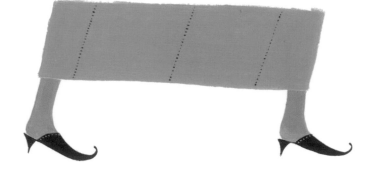

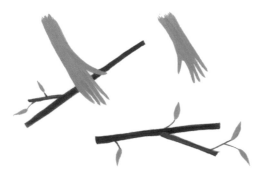

'Oh no, you're not!' thought the princess, but how could she escape?

They flew all day until sunset. Then, as orange rays of sunlight bathed the evening sky, the magician brought them down to land in a rich green pasture near a forest. There, he ordered the princess to gather firewood while he rested near his beloved ebony horse.

Shams el Nahar went into the forest and started gathering branches and twigs. Luckily for her, the King of Greece was riding by, on his return from a hunting expedition. He was intrigued when he saw a beautiful woman dressed in strange and expensive robes gathering wood like a peasant. Dismounting from his horse, he bowed low, introduced himself and asked the princess if she needed help. In a low voice, she told him her story, but she was careful not to mention that the ebony horse could fly.

The king sent his guards to seize the magician and carry the ebony horse back to his palace while he rode ahead with the princess. When they reached the palace, he gave her an entire wing of her own and provided many attendants to wait on her. As for the magician, he was put in prison. The ebony horse was taken to the treasury.

Shams el Nahar, who was an intelligent young woman, soon realised that the King of Greece had fallen in love with her and was determined to make her his wife. So she resolved to play a trick on him and pretend she was mad. When the servants came for her the next morning, she started pulling her hair, tearing her fine clothes and throwing her jewellery around the room. But the king said he would wait until she got better, for he was deeply smitten.

Back in Persia, when Kamar el Akmar found out that his beloved Shams el Nahar and his precious ebony horse had both disappeared from the summer palace, he set out to search for them. For weeks he rode through the towns and villages of his father's kingdom, asking

everyone he met whether they had seen an ebony horse or a beautiful princess. But they seemed to have disappeared like a mirage in the sand.

The young prince grew sadder and sadder after each place he visited, but he never gave up hope of finding his beloved princess. Then one day, while he was sitting in a tavern on the shores of the Mediterranean Sea, he heard some sailors talk about a mad princess who had come to Greece on a strange wooden horse. The king who had found her, they said, was asking all the doctors in the land to cure her so that he could marry her. He was offering one of his palaces in reward.

For the first time in months, Kamar el Akmar smiled. Within moments he had made a plan. He decided to disguise himself as a learned doctor and present himself to the king.

'Who are you and where do you come from?' asked the King of Greece when the prince was brought before him.

'I am a learned Persian doctor and I travel the world curing people,' answered Kamar el Akmar. 'I have heard of the princess's illness and the great reward you are offering, so I thought I would offer you my services.'

'She is the most beautiful woman I have ever set eyes on,' said the king, 'but alas, ever since I decided to marry her she has been most uncontrollable. She came with a strange ebony horse, which I have deposited in my treasury, and an ugly old man whom she said had abducted her — he is in my dungeons. If you can help, I shall be forever in your debt, young man.'

'May I have a look at this horse, your majesty?' Kamar el Akmar asked. 'I feel it may be part of the reason for her unfortunate condition.'

When the wooden horse was brought from the treasury, Kamar el Akmar discreetly tweaked its right ear and its left to check whether the horse was still in perfect working order. 'Hum, hum,' he said to the king. 'In my opinion, the horse and the princess are both under a spell. May I be permitted to see the patient alone?'

When Kamar el Akmar entered the chamber of Shams el Nahar, the princess did not recognise him. So she began to moan and groan and writhe about on her bed. Then Kamar el Akmar approached her gently and whispered his name in her ear. At that, the princess uttered a loud cry as if seized by a fit and fell silent.

'Everyone must now leave the room,' cried the so-called doctor. 'This young lady needs to be left alone.' At this, the maidservants all withdrew in a flutter of slippers and veils.

'My darling, you have been so clever,' said Kamar el Akmar when everyone had gone. 'Your trick has saved you from getting married to this king.'

'We must find a way to get out of here,' said Shams el Nahar, 'before they discover you are not a real doctor.'

'You must pretend that you are getting better,' said Kamar el Akmar, 'but not fully cured, so that I can still see you.'

Everyone rejoiced to see the foreign princess looking and feeling so much better, especially the king.

'I believe, your majesty,' said the doctor, 'that the princess is possessed by a genie who resides in the wooden horse. The way to cure this affliction is to take them both to the pasture where you first found them so that I can perform a ritual and free them of this evil spirit.'

The grateful king arranged for the entire court to come along and watch the proceedings. When they reached the spot where the princess had been found, Kamar el Akmar told the king: 'Your majesty, I shall first light a circle of fire around the horse to burn herbs and incense and chase away the evil genie living inside it. Do not be alarmed when you see the horse rocking backwards and forwards, for it will be trying to get rid of the genie.'

'Do what needs to be done,' answered the king, unable to think about anything except the princess, who would soon be his bride.

'Your majesty,' added Kamar el Akmar, 'I must also advise you that the princess has to be seated on the horse when I chant my incantations.'

'Do your job the best way you can,' said the king, 'and you will be handsomely rewarded.'

'Oh! Just one last thing, your majesty,' said Kamar el Akmar. 'I too need to be on the horse, in case it throws the princess off its back.'

'Yes, yes!' said the king. 'Let's get this over and done with.'

So Kamar el Akmar sprang on to the horse's back behind Shams el Nahar, rode it into the flames and twisted its right ear. The horse rocked back and forth and started slowly rising off the ground. The king and his guards could not see what was happening behind the smoke, but suddenly one of them shouted: 'Your majesty, look up, look up, the horse is flying away!'

'Come back here this instant!' shouted the king. 'Guards, draw your bows!'

But it was too late. The ebony horse was already flying through the sky like a great bird, carrying the lovers back to Persia. This time, Kamar el Akmar took no risks; he landed right in front of his father's palace.

The whole city rejoiced at the return of their prince and his beautiful bride.

The shah organised his son's wedding feast that same night. The festivities lasted for forty days and forty nights, during which time an envoy was sent to the King of Sanaa informing him of his daughter's safe return and her marriage to the Persian prince. With the envoy, Kamar el Akmar also sent an invitation to his father-in-law, asking him to come and visit, together with a casket full of jewels and gold as a sign of good will.

On the final night of the wedding, Shah Sabur slipped away from the festivities and into the stables. And do you know what he did? He broke the levers in the ebony horse's ears to make sure that his son would never be able to ride it again.

'I would have done the same,' said Shahriyar to Shahrazade.

'Why would you have done that, your majesty?' she asked,
in her softest voice.

'Because when one loves someone, one must make sure you keep
them close and safe,' he replied.

'That is true, sire,' said Shahrazade. And when she was certain
the shah was fast asleep, she slipped out of his chambers, thinking
of the story she would tell him the following night to ensure her
own continued safety.

The Speaking Bird and the Singing Tree

One starry night, as Shahrazade was listening to the glorious warbling of the bulbul, Shahriyar called out: 'Shahrazade, what's the matter with you tonight — why are you late with my story?'

'I am listening to the song of the bulbul,' she answered. 'You should listen too, or you may not enjoy the story I am about to tell you...'

The Three Sisters

Once upon a time in the land of Persia there lived a shah called Khusrau. Now, this shah liked nothing better than to disguise himself as a pauper and wander the streets after dinner, eavesdropping on his subjects. He believed it to be the only way to discover what was going on in his kingdom.

One evening, as Khusrau was passing through a poor district of the city, he heard three sisters having a lively discussion. He stopped outside the closed shutters of a window and listened to their conversation.

'I wish I was married to the shah's baker,' said one voice. 'I would have freshly baked bread every morning and invite my friends for tea and cakes every afternoon.'

'I wish I was married to the shah's cook,' said a second voice. 'I would have delicious stews at lunchtime and invite my friends for sumptuous dinners.'

'I wish I was married to the shah himself,' said another voice, the sweetest of the three. 'Then you could both come and live with me in the palace and we would all dress in the nicest clothes and have wonderful parties.'

Khusrau smiled indulgently at these words, then headed back to the palace. But that night he could not sleep. He kept on hearing that voice as sweet as a bulbul's, saying: 'I wish I was married to the shah.'

So the next morning, he called his grand vizier and said: 'Bring those three sisters to the palace immediately.' And he described the exact location of their home. The sisters were in all of a fluster when they arrived. They were even more astounded when the shah said to them: 'Do you remember what you were telling each other last night? Well, it is about to come true.'

'You,' he told the eldest sister, 'will marry my chief baker. And you,' he told the second sister, 'will marry my chief cook. And you, fair one,' he told the youngest sister, with the voice as sweet as a bulbul's, 'you shall marry the shah!'

As no one ever dared argue with a shah, the wedding festivities happened that same night – two weddings in the servants' quarters and the third one in the great hall. This made the older sisters immensely jealous. From that day on they plotted and schemed, determined to destroy their sister's marriage.

The shah was so in love with his young and lovely wife that nothing was good enough for her. He covered her with splendid jewels and silken robes, and he took her with him everywhere he went until she fell pregnant with their first child.

One day while the shah was out hunting, his wife gave birth to a beautiful little boy. Exhausted by the birth, she summoned her older sisters for help. But they did a very evil thing – they took the baby away, wrapped him in a blanket, placed him in a basket and let it float downriver.

When the queen awoke, she found a little puppy sleeping in her bed. 'Look at what our queen has given birth to!' said her sisters, pretending to be astonished.

The shah came back to find his wife in tears. 'I must have married a djinn,' he thought to himself. But he did not dismiss his young wife, as her sisters had hoped. Soon she was heavily pregnant with their second child. This time, she gave birth to another baby boy. Once again,

she called on her older sisters for help. And once again, the older sisters took the baby away, wrapped him in a blanket, placed him in a basket and let it float downriver.

When the queen awoke, she found a little kitten sleeping in her bed. Khusrau's mood turned dark. 'My wife cannot be fully human,' he thought. 'But what can I do? I love her too much; I must give her one last chance.'

And so another year passed and the queen gave birth to a little girl. This time the evil sisters replaced the baby with a small lamb. Like her two brothers before her, the baby was placed in a basket and left to float downriver.

'Enough is enough,' said the angry shah. 'I am sending my wife to a farm, along with her cat, dog and lamb, for that is exactly where she belongs.'

So the poor queen was sent into exile. As for the shah, he was too angry to consider looking for another wife or having any more children. However, Allah in his infinite mercy had other plans. Each of the children was found by the head gardener, who lived at the far end of the palace grounds. He and his wife were childless, so they were overjoyed at the arrival of three beautiful babies. They called the first boy Fareed, which means 'Unique'; the second boy they named Fouad, which means 'Heart'; and the baby girl they called Feyrouz, which means 'Turquoise'.

Fareed, Fouad and Feyrouz grew up in the care of the head gardener and his wife, who ensured that the children were brought up well and were given a fine education. When the gardener and his wife grew old, the shah, in appreciation of his long and excellent service, gave his former servant a country house with enough land to design his ideal garden. The head gardener turned his plot into a small paradise, with gurgling fountains and exotic plants, shady trees and meandering paths. There the family spent some very precious days together.

But all good things come to an end and after a few years the head gardener and his wife passed away. The children became even closer now. Fareed and Fouad took great care of Feyrouz, and she made it her task to look after her father's garden the way he would have wanted.

One day, as Fareed and Fouad were out hunting, an old woman stopped by the house asking for shade and water. Touched by her suffering, Feyrouz took her into the house, offered her refreshment and invited her to rest under the boughs of her favourite cedar. When the old woman awoke from her sleep, she thanked Feyrouz and asked her for a tour of the garden. Feyrouz happily obliged, telling her guest all about the plants, the trees, the birds and the fountains. The old woman did not utter a word, just nodding her head now and then in response.

'So, good woman,' asked Feyrouz at last, 'what do you think of my father's garden?'

The old woman cleared her throat and said: 'Well, my dear child, this is indeed one of the most beautiful gardens I have ever seen. However, if I may be frank, there are a few things missing from it.'

'Missing!' exclaimed Feyrouz. 'What can be missing?'

'Your garden will never be complete without three essential elements, my dear,' replied the old woman. 'What your garden truly needs is a speaking bird, a singing tree and golden water.'

'And how will I find this bird and this tree and this water?' asked Feyrouz.

'Anyone who follows the road from your house and walks for twenty days can find these marvellous items if, on the twentieth day, they ask the first person they meet about them,' said the old woman. And with these words, she took her leave of Feyrouz and went on her way.

When Fareed and Fouad returned that evening, Feyrouz was silent and preoccupied; quite unlike her usual talkative self.

'Is something bothering you, dear Feyrouz?' asked her brothers.

'There is,' she answered, 'but I would feel silly telling you.'

They only got the full story after much teasing and cajoling and promising not to laugh at her too much. 'I shall go and find the speaking bird and the singing tree for you tomorrow,' declared Fareed. 'And in case you worry about me, here is my dagger. If any blood appears on it, you will know that I am in grave danger. If not, you may be sure that I am safe.'

Feyrouz secured the dagger to her belt in a silver sheath studded with precious stones. At dawn, Fareed saddled his horse and galloped away, only stopping to sleep, eat and pray. On the twentieth day, he came across an old dervish sitting under a shady tree with a large sack beside him.

'Wise man, can you please tell me where I can find the speaking bird, the singing tree and the golden water?' Fareed enquired.

'Are you aware of the dangers you will have to face to obtain these marvellous items?' the dervish asked.

'I will face any difficulty to make my sister Feyrouz happy,' replied Fareed.

'Then listen carefully,' said the dervish, reaching into his sack and bringing out a round metal bowl. 'Take this bowl and throw it in front of you. Let it roll until it stops. Ride your horse to the exact place where the bowl lands. Dismount from your horse and leave the bridle over its neck. It will wait for you in the same place until you return. As you go up the hill, you will see to right

95

and left a great quantity of black stones. Don't stop. You will also hear voices making all kinds of unpleasant comments. Don't turn your head to look behind or you will instantly be transformed into a black stone. If you reach the top of the mountain without looking back, you will see a cage with the bird you seek,' continued the dervish.

'What about the singing tree and the golden water?' asked Fareed.

'Ask the speaking bird and he will tell you where to find them,' replied the old man.

'Thank you, wise one,' said Fareed.

'May Allah protect you, young man,' said the dervish.

So Fareed mounted his horse and threw the bowl as far as he could. The bowl rolled for a long time until it stopped at the foot of a mountain scattered with black stones. He dismounted, left the bridle over the horse's neck and began to climb. He had barely walked a few steps when the voices that the old dervish had warned him of began to whisper in his ear: 'Where are you going, you fool? What do you want from this mountain?'

Other voices shouted: 'Stop thief! Stop! Go back home! There is no speaking bird here!' Other voices shouted: 'Kill him, catch him, quarter him!' while others answered: 'No, don't touch him, leave him alone, do not hurt him!'

Ignoring all the voices, Fareed climbed up and up until the voices became so strong they gave him a headache. His hands started sweating and his knees trembling.

'What's the matter with me?' he thought. 'I am feeling so weak I don't think I can carry on. I'd better turn back.' But the moment he turned his head, he was transformed into a black stone. Down at the bottom of the mountain, his horse became a black stone as well.

Feyrouz the Brave

Feyrouz, who had been regularly checking the dagger Fareed had given her, pulled it out of its sheath that evening to find it covered in blood. She was so horrified that she threw the dagger away and started sobbing inconsolably. Fouad heard his sister's sobs and ran to see what was the matter. At the sight of the bloodied dagger on the floor, he put his arms around Feyrouz to console her.

'It's my fault,' she cried. 'I wish I had never listened to that old witch!'

'I know how much you want that bird,' said Fouad. 'So I shall fetch it for you and find out what has happened to our dear brother as well.'

'Please don't go, dear Fouad!' Feyrouz begged. 'I could not bear it if anything happened to you as well.'

But her brother wouldn't be swayed. 'How will I know if you are safe?' asked Feyrouz, knowing it was useless to argue with him.

'Take my amber worry beads,' said Fouad. 'Run them through your fingers several times a day. If they run smoothly, I am safe; if they stop moving on their thread, I am in grave danger.'

Feyrouz took the worry beads and wrapped them several times around her wrist. Then she kissed her brother goodbye and retired to her room to pray for his safe return.

After twenty days of hard riding, Fouad met the same old dervish that Fareed had met, sitting under the shade of the same tree. 'Peace be with you, wise one,' he said. 'Can you please tell me where I can find the speaking bird, the singing tree and the golden water?'

'A young man who looked very much like you asked me this question not so long ago,' answered the dervish.

'It must have been my brother,' said Fouad.

'Poor young man,' sighed the dervish. 'He must now be one of those numerous stones scattered on that mountain.'

'And how does one reach the mountain?' asked Fouad.

'I wish I did not know,' said the dervish gloomily. 'But the truth has to be told and travellers have to be helped.'

He then took a round metal bowl from the sack he had next to him and gave Fouad exactly the same instructions that he had given Fareed.

Fouad threw the bowl as far as he could. It rolled for a long time and stopped at the foot of the mountain scattered with black stones. There Fouad dismounted, hugged his horse and stood for a while gathering his courage, determined that he would reach the top. He had barely walked a few steps, however, when the voice of a man shouted behind him: 'Stop thief, you're trespassing on my mountain!'

Without thinking, Fouad turned his head to speak to the man, but was instantly transformed into a black stone, together with his horse.

Poor Feyrouz! When she ran the amber beads through her fingers that afternoon, they were stiff and heavy. She knew then that Fouad was in grave danger. This time, she did not even waste time crying. Instead, she went into her brother's room, took some of his clothes, disguised herself as a man, jumped on her favourite horse and rode for twenty days to the place where the old dervish lived.

The Speaking Bird and the Singing Tree

Alighting from her horse, she asked the old man: 'Good uncle, have you seen two handsome young men looking for the speaking bird and the singing tree?'

'You must be the exceptional young woman they were trying to please,' said the old dervish, smiling. 'Nothing could disguise your beautiful voice.'

'I beg you, good uncle, to help me find them,' pleaded Feyrouz.

'They came to me a while ago and I gave them the same instructions that I will give you,' said the old man, reaching into his sack. 'Take this bowl and throw it as far as it goes and when it stops, you must stop, leave your horse and climb the mountain. The difficult part is to resist the voices that will shout at you from the mountain.'

'How can I resist them?' asked Feyrouz anxiously.

'You must have a quiet mind and the eyes of a falcon fixed on its prey,' the dervish answered. 'And you must never look behind you or you will be transformed into a black stone.'

'I can be like a falcon,' said Feyrouz, 'I have gone hunting with my brothers numerous times and have observed these princely birds fixing their prey. But how do I quiet my mind?'

'By ignoring the voices,' replied the dervish.

'I have an idea,' said Feyrouz. 'I will stuff my ears with scraps of cloth.'

'Splendid idea,' said the dervish, smiling. He had not smiled for many years, but seeing a beautiful and courageous young woman determined to save those she loved moved the old man, bringing tears to his eyes. 'Remember the falcon!' he said. 'Focus on your goal and don't look back!'

'Thank you for the good advice,' said Feyrouz, jumping on her horse and throwing the bowl in front of her as far as it would roll. 'Remember the falcon,' she repeated to herself.

Feyrouz then calmly climbed the mountain, looking neither right nor left and not hearing the cacophony of voices, which grew louder with every step. She kept her gaze focused on the mountain top until she could see in the distance the cage with the speaking bird in it. As if from

afar, for she still had the pieces of cloth in her ears, she heard the speaking bird say: 'Stop – don't move, don't come any closer.'

But Feyrouz was determined to get hold of that cage, so she ran the last few yards with her eyes fixed on the bird. 'I've got you!' she shouted, grabbing the handle. 'Now you're mine!' The moment Feyrouz took hold of the cage, the bird inside it started singing so she took the pieces of cloth out of her ears to hear him. Feyrouz was enchanted, but she knew her work was not yet over. 'Tell me where to find the singing tree,' she asked.

'Turn around and you will see a wood with the singing tree right in the middle of it,' said the bird. 'You will recognise it immediately. You need only take a branch of the tree to plant in your garden.'

The moment Feyrouz entered the wood, she saw a magnificent tree overshadowing the others with its impressive height. 'I don't think I have ever heard such a beautiful tune,' she thought to herself as she listened to the exquisite tinkling of its leaves. Then, approaching the tree, she begged its pardon as she carefully broke off one of its lower branches. Returning with the branch to the speaking bird, she asked him: 'Now I need you to please tell me how to find the golden water.'

'That's simple,' said the bird in his beautiful voice. 'If you sit still for a while, you will hear the sound of a gurgling stream. Just follow the sound and you will see the golden water.'

Following the bird's instructions, Feyrouz found the stream. It was glistening in the sun with all the colours of the rainbow. The golden water rippling over the stones of the riverbed was as bright as shooting stars on a summer night. 'This is truly one of the most beautiful sights I have ever seen,' said Feyrouz to herself as she filled a small flask she had brought with her.

'I have one more task to accomplish,' said Feyrouz when she had returned to the singing bird, 'and that is to find my brothers.'

'Sprinkle a drop of golden water over every black stone you encounter on your way down the hill,' the bird advised, 'and among them you will find your brothers.'

Feyrouz made her way down the hill, sprinkling drops of golden water on every black stone she passed. The moment a drop of the water touched a stone, it turned into either a human being or a horse. Soon, dozens of young men were stretching their limbs and yawning as if waking from a long sleep, and horses were neighing and shaking their manes and limbs. When Feyrouz finally reached the stones that were her brothers, transforming them with the magic water, all three of them wept tears of joy at being reunited. They then joined what was by now a small battalion of men and horses.

One by one, each man and his horse left the group and went on their way, until only Feyrouz and her brothers remained. Returning home, they hung the cage of the speaking bird by a pergola covered with golden and purple grapes, and they planted the branch of the singing tree in the middle of the garden, where it took root and grew to become the most beautiful tree of all. They then poured the golden water into one of the fountains where it surged in beautiful glistening jets, splashing and sparkling by day and by night. And it looked as if they would all live happily ever after in their beautiful house and garden.

The Eyes of the Heart

The news of the garden with the speaking bird, singing tree and golden water spread far and wide. Many people asked permission to see these wonders with their own eyes. Feyrouz was a graceful, kind and patient hostess, who greatly enjoyed showing her father's garden to her many visitors. Seeing their sister happily occupied in this way, Fareed and Fouad returned to their favourite pastime: hunting.

One day, as the brothers were riding in pursuit of a fox, they came upon Shah Khusrau's hunting party. 'May the blessings of Allah and his Prophet be upon you, your majesty,' said the two brothers, dismounting and prostrating themselves before the shah.

'Who are you, young men?' asked Khusrau, strangely stirred by this encounter.

'We are the sons of your late head gardener,' replied Fareed, 'and it would please us enormously if you were to pay a visit to our father's garden.'

'Indeed!' exclaimed the shah. 'I have heard fascinating stories about your garden and its speaking bird. It would please me immensely to see it.'

'We could not have wished for a greater honour,' said Fouad. 'Would your majesty care to honour us with his presence tomorrow?'

When the shah agreed, the brothers rushed to their sister to tell her the good news. 'I wish mother was here,' said Feyrouz with tears in her eyes. 'I have no idea how to entertain a shah.'

'Why don't we ask the speaking bird?' suggested Fareed.

'That's an excellent idea' replied Feyrouz, rushing to the garden. 'Speaking bird! O speaking bird,' she asked, 'what does one feed a shah?' And the bird replied:

Shahs like nothing better than eating baked cucumber
Stuffed with fresh pearls on toasted bread and butter.

'You mean stuffed with rice, surely?' said Feyrouz.

'No, I mean pearls,' answered the speaking bird.

The following day, as a big fanfare announced the arrival of the shah, Feyrouz and her brothers rushed to greet him. Bowing down before him, they then led him to the garden and invited him to sit under the pergola while the speaking bird sang a tune of welcome.

After taking some refreshment, they showed Khusrau the fountain where the golden water tumbled and splashed. 'This is truly a wonderful sight,' said the shah. Then, turning to Feyrouz, he asked her to lead him to the singing tree. As she walked ahead, he could not help but admire her graceful demeanour, her elegant dress and her delicate hands. It was a pity he could not see her face for she had covered it, so that only her eyes were visible.

'How lucky my head gardener was to have such wonderfully handsome and loving children,' Khusrau thought to himself. 'Why did I have to have such bad luck and be given a cat, a puppy and a lamb instead?' Out loud, he enquired of Feyrouz: 'What age are you, my child?'

'Sixteen years old, sire,' she replied.

'That's the age my youngest child would have been,' thought Khusrau. But his musings were interrupted by a melody so enchanting that he believed Feyrouz and her brothers must have

hired an orchestra for his visit and hidden it in the garden. 'This is such beautiful music,' he said to his young hostess. 'I must congratulate the musicians.'

'The music is made by the singing tree, sire,' explained Feyrouz. 'It changes with the time of day and the weather. The tunes become sad when it is cold and happy when it is warm. The tree is quiet during the night and vivacious during the day. No tune is ever the same.'

'How lucky you are to have such treasures in your garden,' replied the shah. 'You must count your blessings every day.'

'Indeed we do, sire,' replied Feyrouz.

'This music and the walk have whetted my appetite,' declared the shah. 'Let's see if your cook can conjure up a meal as exquisite as the music of this tree!'

The meal was served under the pergola by the cage of the speaking bird. But you should have seen the shah's face when he realised that the cucumbers were stuffed with pearls! 'What is this?' he cried angrily. 'Are you trying to poison me?'

Before the brothers or their sister could answer, the speaking bird piped up:

> *Why is it such a surprise to see cucumbers stuffed with pearls?*
> *Didn't your majesty surmise when your wife gave birth to animals*
> *That she was somewhat diabolical?*

'That is what her sisters told me,' answered the shah, visibly shaken.

'And why did you believe these old witches?' sang the bird.

'Because I saw the animals with my own eyes,' answered the shah.

'The eyes of the heart are the only eyes that truly see,' said the bird. Then he added:

*Look around you and look afresh
At your beautiful sons and daughter,
Blood of your blood and flesh of your flesh.*

Upon hearing these words, Khusrau's heart melted with joy. Was it possible that he was a father after all? When he looked at the smiling faces of Fouad and Fareed, he saw with his heart's eyes and felt deep in his soul that these were truly his children. He stood up to embrace his sons; then he gently lifted the veil from his daughter's face. She looked exactly like her mother!

'I have been such a fool,' said the shah, 'to have believed those two witches. They have deprived me all these years of the joys of fatherhood.' Then, turning to the speaking bird, he asked: 'Can you tell us the whole story?'

So the speaking bird told the shah how the head gardener had found the three children as babies, each floating down the stream in a basket; how he had given them the best upbringing and education and taught them how to care for and love each other.

Khusrau rose to embrace his children one more time and told them: 'Come, let us mount our horses and ride to the farm where your mother lives. I need to beg for her forgiveness and bring her back to the palace. Then we can be a proper family at long last.'

You should have seen the joyful tears that fell from the face of the exiled queen and the kisses she gave to her long-lost children. You should have heard the sighs they all made at the wasted years and the cries of joy that greeted the royal family when they returned to the palace. You should have seen the rice that was thrown over them by the cheering onlookers and the rose petals carpeting the floor. You should have seen the faces of the two evil sisters when they were thrown into the dungeons, kicking and screaming and protesting their innocence.

And you should have seen the magnificent new cage that was made for the speaking bird out of gold filigree studded with precious stones. It hung in the palace courtyard, shaded by trees whose leafy branches attracted all manner of birds, forming an exquisite choir that delighted everyone who heard it.

'What about the singing tree and the golden water?' asked Shahriyar.

'They remained in the garden of the country house, which Feyrouz and her brothers often visited,' replied Shahrazade.

'It would be wonderful to own such treasures,' sighed the shah. And he remained silent for a while, dreaming of the beautiful music a singing tree and a speaking bird would make.

Prince Kamar el Zaman and Princess Boudour

One evening, Shahrazade ordered her maids to serve supper in the palace gardens, in a tent lit by the full moon.

'I wanted your majesty to look at this magnificent full moon while having dinner,' she explained to the shah. 'Because my story tonight is about two beautiful people who were named after it.'

The Mysterious Lady

Long ago, in a faraway country, lived a king who had everything a king might want – rich and fertile lands, coffers full of gold, a mighty army, four lovely wives and many faithful friends. But the one thing this king did not have was a child. Then, after many prayers and pilgrimages to holy places, the king was given a son so perfect and beautiful that he called him Kamar el Zaman, meaning 'Time's Moon'. The king and his wife couldn't stop looking at him and thanking Allah for their good fortune.

Not only was Kamar el Zaman beautiful but he was studious as well, learning mathematics, history and geography in addition to Arabic and Persian poetry. He was also an accomplished poet himself, a fine calligrapher and a master chess player. Finally, he was an excellent horseman and could ride like the wind.

When Kamar el Zaman had reached the age of eighteen, the king thought of retiring and handing his son the throne.

'Listen, your majesty,' said the grand vizier when the king spoke to him about his plans. 'I agree that Kamar el Zaman is destined to be a great king. But it is much better to find him a wife first. A good woman will advise and support him and make him an even better ruler.'

'What wise words you speak,' said the king. 'Let us tell Kamar el Zaman of our decision.'

How surprised both men were to see Kamar el Zaman's face darken on hearing what they planned. 'I will not even think of marriage before the age of twenty-one,' he told his father.

So the king and the grand vizier waited three

years before broaching the subject again. But again Prince

Kamar el Zaman resisted their proposal: 'I'm not interested in

marriage!'

'I have been too soft with him,' sighed the king. 'I have waited three

years for him to make up his mind about his bride and he still says no.

Guards!' he bellowed. 'Take my son to the tower and lock him up for a week

with only water and rice to feed him and the Koran for company.'

What the king did not know was that the tower, which he believed to

be deserted, was built on the foundations of an old well and that inside

the well lived a lady djinn, Maymouna. This djinn was both powerful and

beautiful and a creature of the night. The moment the moon rose, she would fly

out of the well to meet up with other creatures of the dark.

One evening, as she glided through the night air, Maymouna noticed a light flickering

in the tower. Swooping down to investigate, she flew straight in through the window

and almost woke Kamar el Zaman from his sleep when she lifted the silken coverlet

to take a look at him. 'Praise be to Allah the Creator!' she exclaimed. 'I have never

seen such a handsome human being in all my life.'

Without further thought, Maymouna placed two kisses on Kamar el Zaman's rosy

cheeks and another on his forehead, looked at him for a few minutes longer and then

flew to meet her friends. She was so taken by the young man's beauty that she almost

reached the edge of the world without noticing. But she was jolted back to reality when she bumped into one of the ugliest creatures of the dark, a djinn called Dandache, who had huge black wings and dark eyes.

'You wouldn't believe what has just happened to me,' said Maymouna.

'And you wouldn't believe what has just happened to me either,' replied Dandache. 'I have just returned from China, where I have seen the most beautiful princess in the world. Her name is Boudour, and she is indeed as radiant as the moon after which she is named. She has hair as long and lustrous as a horse's tail, eyes as brown as a chestnut and lips as full as a rose in bloom. She is no ordinary princess either – her father loves her so much that he has had seven palaces built specially for her: one for each day of the week.'

'Is that all?' asked Maymouna, somewhat annoyed at being so upstaged.

'No, it is not,' replied Dandache. 'The king is desperate for his daughter to marry so he can have grandchildren but the beautiful princess has refused every suitor who has presented himself, however rich, brave or handsome.'

'So what?' replied Maymouna. 'Marriage may not be for her.'

'That may be the case,' answered Dandache. 'What is extraordinary is that the princess has saddened her father very much by threatening to kill herself if he presents her with yet another man. As a result, the king has ordered her to be locked away in one of her seven palaces, guarded night and day by her old nurse, who knows every trick a young girl might think of. I happen to live near this palace,'

Dandache went on, 'and every night when the princess is fast asleep, I fly through her window and kiss her on both cheeks.'

'This is an amazing story,' conceded Maymouna, 'because it is the very mirror of mine. I have just met the most handsome prince I have ever seen. He too has been locked away by his father and is sleeping soundly as we speak.'

'I bet you that my princess is more beautiful than your prince,' taunted Dandache.

'You don't know what you are talking about!' snorted Maymouna.

'Then bring him to China so we can compare the two,' suggested Dandache.

'No, you bring her here!' insisted Maymouna.

As the more powerful of the two djinns, in the end she had her way. Dandache spread his huge black wings and flew straight back to China to bring his princess to the tower where Kamar el Zaman slept so peacefully.

Dandache gently deposited the princess next to the prince and both djinns gazed at the two mortals for a while in silence, quite unable to decide who was the more beautiful of the two. Then Maymouna had an idea: 'Let's wake them up and see which one expresses greater admiration for the other.'

'Perfect,' agreed Dandache.

So Maymouna transformed herself into a flea and nibbled Kamar el Zaman on the neck. He woke up with a cry, swatting his neck and looking around to catch the culprit. The first thing he saw was the Chinese princess.

'I must be dreaming,' he thought, rubbing his eyes. 'Who is this divine creature lying by my side?' He took her hand and tried to rouse her, but Dandache had placed a spell on the princess and she did not stir. 'Maybe this is the young woman my father had in mind for a bride,' thought the prince. 'Maybe that's why he was so upset when I kept refusing to get married. Now I understand his anger.'

Then, lifting the princess's hand, he saw that she was wearing an exquisite ring of golden filigree. 'Let me put her ring on my finger so that I can show both her and my father the seriousness of my intentions,' for he had fallen instantly in love with her. Then, feeling suddenly overwhelmed with sleep, he lay back in his bed and dozed off.

It was now Dandache's turn. He transformed himself into a gnat and bit the princess on her big toe. 'Ouch!' she cried. 'What was that?'

Of course, she too was startled to find herself not alone but lying beside the most handsome young man she had ever seen. Then she noticed her ring on his little finger. 'How did that get there?' she wondered. She took the stranger's hand and shook it hard, but Maymouna's spell was so strong that he did not so much as blink!

'Oh well,' she sighed. 'Maybe he will be awake in the morning and then I can ask him why my ring is on his finger!' Then, feeling suddenly weary, she too drifted back to sleep.

'Now,' said Maymouna to Dandache, 'which is more handsome? My prince or your princess?'

Dandache had to concede that Kamar el Zaman's beauty was difficult to beat, so he offered to take the princess back to her palace.

In the morning, the first thing Kamar el Zaman did upon waking was to look for the beautiful young woman he had seen beside him during the night. 'I cannot believe she has disappeared!' he cried. 'I hope this is not yet another of my father's tricks.' So he called the guard outside the door and asked him: 'Where is the beautiful lady who was in my room last night?'

'Our prince is starting to hallucinate all alone in this tower,' said the guard to himself. Out loud, he answered the prince politely: 'Lady? What lady? There was no lady, beautiful or otherwise, in your room last night, your highness, or I would have noticed.'

'You haven't noticed a thing!' said the prince, getting angry. 'There was a lady in my room last night. Indeed, I have her ring to prove it!'

The guard did not know how to answer the prince, so he rushed to the king to tell him that his son was having hallucinations and that he should be taken out of the tower at once. The king sent the grand vizier to the tower immediately in order to question his son. Upon hearing about the lady, the vizier said: 'How could she have entered your room, your highness, without disturbing the guard?'

'If she wasn't here, where did I get this ring from?' answered Kamar el Zaman angrily. 'Go and tell my father that she was indeed here last night and that she is the only one I will ever marry!'

So the grand vizier rushed back to the king but with more questions than answers. This time the king himself came to the tower and questioned his son about the mysterious lady.

'I assure you, father, that there was a lady in my chamber last night and this ring is my proof. I beg you to find her because she is the only one I will ever marry!' And with these words the prince took to his bed, refusing all food.

The king was beside himself with worry and called his council to discuss the matter.

The Lost Prince

In the meantime, far away in the land of China, Princess Boudour woke up to find herself back in her room with no handsome prince by her side. 'Nurse!' she called. 'Where is the young man I saw last night?'

'Young man? What young man, my dear?' answered the old woman, pressing her hand on the princess's forehead to check whether the girl was feverish.

'The young man who took my ring,' answered the princess.

'But, my dear child, we left you alone last night and there was no way anyone could have entered your room!' said the nurse.

'I tell you that my ring has disappeared. See!' she said, showing her bare fingers.

'I'm calling your mother,' answered the nurse, who was now quite agitated.

'Darling,' said the queen, 'you must have misplaced your ring in the bath or when you were undressing for bed. Besides, no young man would dare enter your private quarters, let alone your room, without permission.'

'Mother, if you don't believe me I will stay in bed and refuse all food until you find the young man in question, because he is the one I wish to marry!'

So the queen rushed out of her daughter's room and went to her husband. The king called his councillors and said: 'Announce to everyone that whoever cures my daughter of her madness will be given her hand in marriage.'

Doctors, magicians, astrologers and wise men of every kind were called to the princess's bedside, but no one could find a cure.

Prince Kamar el Zaman and Princess Boudour

Now, the princess's nurse had a son called Marzavan. He was the same age as Boudour and was like a brother to her as they had grown up together in the palace. He had spent the last few years travelling to many countries in order to sit at the feet of famous sages, and he had just returned to China full of wisdom and new ideas. On hearing that Boudour was unwell, he rushed to her bedside. She was so happy to see him that she opened her heart to him at once and told him her strange story.

'I believe you, sister,' he said. 'And I am going to find this young man and bring him to you.'

Marzavan travelled for many months across mountains and deserts, by horse and by ship, until he reached the country where Kamar el Zaman lived. Here, he heard the story of the young prince pining for a young woman he had once seen in a dream.

'This sounds promising!' he thought to himself. And he went immediately to the capital city and asked for an audience with the king. By now, the king was prepared to try anything, so he took his exotic visitor straight to his son's sleeping quarters. Marzavan looked at the prince lying on his bed, eyes half closed, then leaned down towards him and whispered in his ear: 'I know the lady you are looking for. She is Princess Boudour, daughter of Gaiour, King of China, and she has sent me to you.'

Kamar el Zaman's eyes flew open. He tried to sit up in his bed, but he was too weak.

'Let me help, your highness,' said Marzavan propping up the pillows.

'Describe this princess to me,' said Kamar el Zaman.

So Marzavan told the prince about Princess Boudour – radiant as the moon, with hair as long and lustrous as a horse's tail, eyes as brown as a chestnut and lips as full as a rose in bloom.

'It's her! It's her!' cried Kamar el Zaman. 'Bring me some chicken soup and bread,' he commanded his servants. 'I am absolutely starving!'

'You must regain your strength fast,' said Marzavan.

'Why?' asked Kamar el Zaman between small mouthfuls.

'Because I promised to take you to her,' Marzavan replied.

A week later, Kamar el Zaman told his father that he was going hunting with his new friend. 'We shall be gone for a few days,' he told the king, 'so that I can show him the region.'

So Kamar el Zaman and Marzavan took two horses each, one for riding and the other for carrying provisions, as well as two grooms to tend the horses. They set off early in the morning and rode all day. When evening came, they stopped at a caravanserai for food and rest. While the grooms were asleep, Marzavan asked Kamar el Zaman to give him one of his shirts, offering one of his own in return. Then he went to the stables and brought out three of the four horses.

'Let's go now,' whispered Marzavan. 'But very quietly, so as not to wake anyone.'

The young men rode all night, with one horse in tow, until they reached a forest. 'Do not judge me badly for what I am about to do,' said Marzavan to Kamar el Zaman. With these words, he drew his sword and killed the spare horse.

'Why have you killed the horse?' cried Kamar el Zaman. 'What has it done to deserve this terrible fate?'

'I had to, my lord,' said Marzavan. Then he took the shirt Kamar el Zaman had given him earlier, tore it up and dipped it in the horse's blood, leaving it lying on the ground.

'What are you doing now?' cried Kamar el Zaman in alarm.

'We need to mislead your father's men about your whereabouts. You see, when the grooms wake up and discover that we have gone, they will raise the alarm. Your father will send his troops to look for you. When they find the dead horse and the torn shirt, they will believe you have been killed by bandits or wild animals and stop looking for you.'

'This is a cruel trick to play on an old man,' protested Kamar el Zaman.

'I know it is,' said Marzavan. 'But this is the only way you can travel freely to see your beloved Princess Boudour.'

'I suppose you're right,' sighed Kamar el Zaman. 'Poor father, I can see his sad face already. At the same time, I cannot wait to introduce him to my darling Boudour.'

So the young men mounted their horses and left the forest, travelling by land and sea through mountains, steppes and plains, until they reached China. 'Let us stop at an inn for a day or so,' said Marzavan. 'We need to find you an astrologer's robe.'

'You never cease to amaze me!' exclaimed Kamar el Zaman. 'Why do I need such a thing?'

'The only way you can enter the king's palace is to pretend to be an astrologer,' replied Marzavan. 'For King Gaiour has called upon every wise man in this land and beyond to see if he can find a cure for his beloved daughter. Are you ready to act like one?'

'I'll do anything to see the princess again,' said Kamar el Zaman.

'Listen to me in that case,' Marzavan went on. 'When you reach the palace gates, you will claim to be a famous astrologer from Arabia. In the meantime, I will go into the palace and give my mother a note to take to Princess Boudour.'

When two days had passed and the astrologer's robe had been purchased, Kamar el Zaman made his way to the palace. Upon reaching the gates, he raised his voice and shouted: 'I am the astrologer of astrologers, and I have come all the way from Arabia to cure your beloved princess!'

'Another body for the dungeons,' thought the palace guards, for the penalty for not succeeding was to be thrown in prison.

'So, young man,' asked the king when Kamar el Zaman was brought before him, 'I hear you have a cure for my daughter.'

'I believe I do, your majesty,' replied the prince.

'I cannot believe that such a young man would have the experience needed to cure my beloved daughter,' said the king, looking sceptical.

'Put me to the test,' answered Kamar el Zaman. 'All I need is a quill, ink and paper.'

A portable scribe's desk was brought in and Kamar el Zaman sat down and wrote the following words in his best calligraphic script:

My darling,

Why did you abandon me that night? I have been unable to sleep, eat or enjoy life since you left. Night and day, I think only of you. As a token of my sincere intentions, I return the ring that I took from you that night. This note is not a trick, nor a figment of your imagination. I cannot wait to hold you in my arms at last.

Your loving, pining, desperate Prince Kamar el Zaman

121

Folding the paper, he slipped the ring inside, sealed the letter and gave it to the palace guard.

The princess, who of course had already been warned by Marzavan about Kamar el Zaman's presence in the city, tore open the letter. She did not even have to read the note as she immediately recognised her ring. 'Bring this astrologer to my quarters at once!' she told her nurse. 'I already feel so much better!'

The nurse hurried back to the guard, the guard hurried to the king, and the king hastened to his beloved daughter so that he could see her improved condition for himself. 'The guard did not lie; I can see you are feeling much better. It is a long time since I've seen those pearly white teeth,' said the king, embracing his darling daughter with delight.

'Where is the astrologer?' asked Princess Boudour eagerly.

'He is waiting outside your chambers,' replied the king. 'I am starting to suspect the young man is more than an astrologer – he is clearly a magician of the heart as well.'

'Take me to him, father,' said the princess.

Kamar el Zaman stood transfixed at the sight of his beloved Boudour. He could not move for a few minutes because, despite her recent illness, she looked even more beautiful by day than he had remembered her by night. 'She is worth every mile I have travelled,' he thought as he approached her. Then, kneeling in front of her, he said: 'Here I am at your feet at last.'

The princess smiled as she extended her hand and helped him up, saying to her father: 'Here is the man who has stolen my heart!'

The king laughed, looked at the young couple and said: 'I think it is time I heard your story, young man.'

'I am not really an astrologer, your majesty,' said Kamar el Zaman.

'I suspected as much. Now, let's sit down with a refreshing cup of jasmine tea while you tell me everything.'

'What happened to Marzavan?' asked Shahriyar. 'Was he rewarded
for his efforts?'

'He was given large estates by King Gaiour,' answered Shahrazade.

'Did Kamar el Zaman ever see his father again?' Shahriyar asked,
after a short pause.

'That is another story for another night,' replied Shahrazade with a soft smile.

Seven Nights of Celebrations

When Shahrazade had finished her last story, she said: 'Sire, we have sat together for one thousand and one nights, during which you have heard strange and magical tales and travelled to different worlds. I hope that I have distracted you from your anger and soothed your pain, making you think better of women. Can I now ask for a favour?'

'Why now?' asked Shahriyar.

'I have shared with you the jewels of my imagination and the essence of my wisdom and I have nothing more to give,' answered Shahrazade. 'However, I have one more thing to show you.'

'What is it?' said Shahriyar, intrigued.

'Please wait a moment,' she whispered, leaving the shah's chamber.

A few minutes later, she returned with three little boys, each as beautiful as the morning star: a baby in her arms, a one-year-old crawling on all fours and a two-year-old clinging to her robe.

'These are your children, whom you have never asked to see but who wish to meet you,' she said, bowing to Shahriyar. With this, she placed the baby in his father's arms, while the other two buried their golden-brown heads in her skirts.

'Come on, children, don't be shy,' she said. 'Say good morning to your father.'

There were a few seconds of silence in which neither the boys nor Shahriyar could speak. Then the baby started crying and Shahriyar did not know what to do, so he handed him back clumsily to his mother.

The other two lifted their heads from their mother's robe and looked at their father whose heart leaped with joy at the sight of such beautiful children. Then the elder one said good morning, while the younger smiled like a new moon and babbled in some strange language of his own.

'May I beg you, sire, to think again before killing the mother of your children?' said Shahrazade.

Shahriyar was silent for a few minutes, then he stood up, embraced his wife and said: 'For one thousand and one nights you have kept me company, entertained and amused me, relieved me of my boredom and soothed away my pain and anger. But, more importantly, with your steadfast love you have made me change my mind about the faithlessness of women. You have become as necessary to me as water is to a garden and as a compass is to a sailor.'

Shahrazade hugged her husband with her free arm, the two older boys still clinging to her skirts, and said: 'All I ask from you, sire, is to love them as much as you love yourself.'

'Or as much as I love you, my dear,' said Shahriyar, picking up the one-year-old and bouncing him in the air.

'Me too, father!' cried the two-year-old.

As he picked up his eldest son, Shahriyar turned to his wife and said: 'Allah bless you, my dear, and bless your father and your family and the children you gave me. You are a most perfect wife, intelligent and learned, patient and wise. Your place is beside me on this throne and in my heart.'

At Barefoot Books, we celebrate art and story that opens
the hearts and minds of children from all walks of life, inspiring
them to read deeper, search further, and explore their own creative gifts.
Taking our inspiration from many different cultures, we focus on themes that
encourage independence of spirit, enthusiasm for learning, and sharing of
the world's diversity. Interactive, playful and beautiful, our products
combine the best of the present with the best of the past to
educate our children as the caretakers of tomorrow.

Live Barefoot!
Join us at www.barefootbooks.com

Wafa' Tarnowska

was born in Lebanon, has lived in Australia, India, Cyprus, Poland and the UK, and is currently based in Dubai. In her work, Wafa' strives to create a valuable bridge between East and West, helping to break down the stereotypical images that western peoples have about the East, and vice versa. Wafa' has translated more than a dozen children's books from English to Arabic and is the author of *Dances with the Gods*, a book on Phoenician myths and legends. Wafa' is also the author of *The Seven Wise Princesses* (2000), a retelling for children of the Sufi writer Nizami's medieval classic *Haft Paykar*, praised by *Booklist* as 'A unique offering: multilayered, complex, featuring stories within stories…a real pleasure'.

Carole Hénaff

gains much inspiration from her travels, and is never without her sketchbook. She studied theatrical literature in Paris, before moving to Barcelona to study graphic design and illustration. Now a freelance illustrator, Carole has created images for magazines in many parts of the world. She has illustrated children's books in France and Spain, including *Smara*, which was awarded the Isaac Díaz Pardo prize for Best Illustrated Book, 2006. This is Carole's first project for Barefoot Books.